A Bungalow for Two

Also by Carole Gift Page in Large Print:

In Search of Her Own

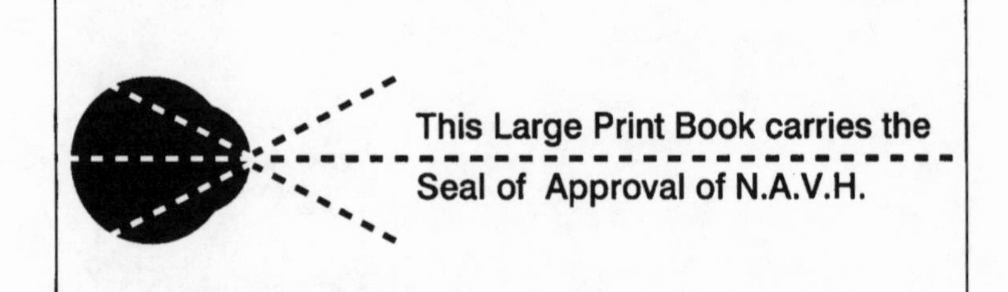

A Bungalow for Two

Carole Gift Page

Thorndike Press • Waterville, Maine

Published in 2003 by arrangement with Harlequin Books S.A.

Thorndike Press® Large Print Christian Romance.

The tree indicium is a trademark of Thorndike Press.

The text of this Large Print edition is unabridged. Other aspects of the book may vary from the original edition.

Set in 16 pt. Plantin by Al Chase.

Printed in the United States on permanent paper.

Library of Congress Cataloging-in-Publication Data

Page, Carole Gift.
A bungalow for two / Carole Gift Page.
p. cm.
ISBN 0-7862-5744-X (lg. print : hc : alk. paper)
1. Women sculptors — Fiction. 2. Seaside resorts — Fiction. 3. Billionaires — Fiction. 4. Recluses — Fiction. 5. Large type books. I. Title.
PS3566.A3326B86 2003
813′.54—dc21 2003054256

In loving memory of
Jason Michael Williams.
February 13, 1981–April 11, 2001
With a heart for God, a passion for life,
great devotion to his family and friends
and an insatiable appetite for adventure,
Jason touched countless lives
in countless ways.
All who knew him loved him.

National Association for Visually Handicapped
serving the partially seeing

As the Founder/CEO of NAVH, the only national health agency solely devoted to those who, although not totally blind, have an eye disease which could lead to serious visual impairment, I am pleased to recognize Thorndike Press* as one of the leading publishers in the large print field.

Founded in 1954 in San Francisco to prepare large print textbooks for partially seeing children, NAVH became the pioneer and standard setting agency in the preparation of large type.

Today, those publishers who meet our standards carry the prestigious "Seal of Approval" indicating high quality large print. We are delighted that Thorndike Press is one of the publishers whose titles meet these standards. We are also pleased to recognize the significant contribution Thorndike Press is making in this important and growing field.

Lorraine H. Marchi, L.H.D.
Founder/CEO
NAVH

* Thorndike Press encompasses the following imprints: Thorndike, Wheeler, Walker and Large Print Press.

No soldier in active service entangles himself in the affairs of everyday life, so that he may please the One who enlisted him as a soldier.

— *2 Timothy* 2:4

Chapter One

Andrew Rowlands was dreaming. An odd dream really. He was about to be married to the lovely Juliana Pagliarulo, but he couldn't find his darling daughters. Surely the wedding couldn't begin without them. He darted among his smiling, well-attired guests, inquiring, "Have you seen my daughters?"

No one had.

And then amid the cacophony of voices and laughter swirling around him, he heard a familiar voice.

"Daddy?"

It was his oldest daughter, Cassandra, in a mauve bridesmaid dress. She came slipping through the crowd with her handsome husband, Antonio, Juliana's son. In her arms Cassie carried a precious bundle, Andrew's first grandson. "Be happy, Daddy," she said, giving him a hug, and squeezing one-month-old Daniel between them.

"I couldn't be happier than I am today, Cassie. I've got all my family around me."

He spotted his second daughter in the throng. His dear Brianna with Eric Wingate, her dashing groom. Beside them stood their soon-to-be-adopted daughter, Charity, looking like an angel in pink chiffon. Andrew strode over and swung the precocious two-year-old up in his arms. "How's my beautiful little Blue Eyes?"

The child tossed back her blond ringlets and laughed. "I not *little,* Gampaw. I big girl!"

Matching her laughter, Andrew kissed her shiny hair, then set her down. "Yes, you certainly are Grandpa's big girl!"

"Oh, Daddy, isn't she the prettiest flower girl you ever saw?" Brianna said in her lyrical voice.

Andrew winked at his daughter. "No prettier than the bride who's going to be her mother."

Brianna swept into Andrew's arms with a tender embrace, her ivory-white wedding gown swishing around her.

"I love you, Daddy," she whispered, stepping back and blowing Andrew a kiss. "Isn't this a glorious day . . . the four of us having a double wedding?"

"Wonderful!" Andrew crooned. "Nothing

better than standing at the altar with my ravishing bride and my precious daughter and her intended."

"We're all going to live happily ever after, Daddy. Happily ever after . . ."

The dream darkened after that. The festive crowd in the wedding chapel receded behind a mist of swirling shadows. A storm was gathering, with voluminous clouds rolling over a shrouded earth. The noise was deafening, drowning out the sounds of celebration rising from the chapel.

"Where's Frannie?" Andrew shouted through the gloom. "Who's seen my youngest daughter?"

The murky darkness cleared, as if someone had pulled back a curtain, and Andrew saw her, his beloved Frannie, who had cared for him like a mother hen. She was dressed in black and kneeling at her mother's grave, the grave of his cherished Mandy, gone seven years now.

Andrew held out a hand to his daughter. "Frannie, come! The wedding's about to begin. Your sisters and I are waiting for you."

She stared back with tears in her eyes. "No, Daddy. I can't! I won't!"

"Honey, please! It won't be the same without you."

"How can you do this, Daddy? How can you forsake Mom and marry a stranger? I'll never forgive you, Daddy!"

"No, Frannie, it's not like that." Andrew reached out, but the shadows closed around his daughter, and she was gone.

"Come back, Frannie! I don't want to lose you, sweetheart . . . !"

Andrew woke in a cold sweat, his heart pounding. Thank goodness, it was just a dream. A silly dream. Everything was okay. Normal as an old shoe. The double wedding had gone off without a hitch nearly two weeks ago, the first of July. And just last night he and Juliana had returned, happy and exhilarated, from their Caribbean honeymoon.

Now he was here in his own home again, surrounded by everything familiar, waking as he always did to the summer sun streaming in his bedroom window. But this time, there was one major exception. Lying in bed next to him was his sleeping bride, the sun casting gold ribbons across her ivory face and bare shoulder.

The warm sunlight reminded him that all was well in his life. Better than it had been in years. He had so much for which to be grateful . . . a devoted wife and two daughters happily married with families of their own.

He had kept his promise to Mandy. "Find our girls good husbands," she had told him during their last hours together. It had been her dying wish. "And find a good woman for yourself, Andrew. You'll need someone to look after you."

Yes, he had done that too. God had given him his exquisite Juliana.

And now, with his two oldest daughters married, that left just one daughter. Frannie, his youngest. A chill rippled though him as he recalled his unsettling dream. Those shadowy, nightmarish images had captured his underlying concern for Frannie. She had taken Mandy's death the hardest. With everyone else in the family married, she seemed so alone, at loose ends, drifting. Surely one of these days the right man would come along for her. It was one of Andrew's most fervent prayers.

And until then, he didn't want Frannie feeling abandoned, just because he had a brand-new family to fuss over. But the truth was, he would have his hands full with his vivacious Juliana and her grown daughter.

If ever a young woman needed a father, it was shy, skittish Belina. She had already endured enough trials and heartaches for a lifetime — the car crash, her father's death, her own disability and disfigurement. But with surgery, counseling and rehabilitation, she had come a long way over the past two years.

Andrew hoped against hope that Frannie would take Belina under her wing and become a real sister to her. Of course, Frannie was stubborn and headstrong and didn't warm to just anybody. She was possessive and overprotective, too, but that was partly Andrew's fault. He had been so needy after Mandy's death, he had allowed his youngest daughter to pamper and mollycoddle him. While he had thrown himself into his ministerial duties at the church, she had taken over the cooking and household chores like a faithful little trooper.

Even when his two older daughters began making lives for themselves, Frannie was the one who dug in her heels and refused to budge. She was going to stay home and take care of her daddy, no matter what. No wonder she had resisted the idea of him bringing home a new bride and stepdaughter.

But Andrew was just as determined as Frannie. With Cassie and Brianna married now and establishing homes of their own, he would encourage Frannie to find in Juliana and Belina the motherly and sisterly companionship she missed.

It was a long shot, to be sure. In temperament, Frannie and Juliana were like oil and water. Add to the mix Belina's reclusive personality, and you had a recipe for trouble. But, as he had learned long ago, with God all things were possible. More than once, Andrew had staked his life on that Scriptural principle.

Another unmistakable reality confronted Andrew. The Rowlands household was going to be a very different place from now on. How drastically it had changed in the past seven years, starting with Mandy's death, then Cassie's marriage, then the double wedding of Andrew and Juliana and Brianna and Eric. And now Brianna had moved out just as Cassie had, and Juliana and his new stepdaughter had moved in.

Andrew rolled over and gazed again at his sleeping bride. Lightly he caressed a strand of her shiny black hair that rippled over the pillow. He yearned to sweep her up in his arms, but she looked so peaceful, he was reluctant to startle her.

It still hardly seemed possible that God had blessed him with two remarkable women in one lifetime. Naturally, Juliana was nothing like Mandy; they were as opposite as night and day. Mandy had been quiet, self-assured, delicate, refined. Juliana was fun-loving, flamboyant, larger than life.

Andrew rested his arms under his head and looked up at the ceiling. Over the years he had grown so accustomed to talking to Mandy in his mind that it was a hard habit to break, even with Juliana lying beside him.

Mandy, he mused with a wry half smile, can you believe it? Here I am with Juliana. My wife. She isn't like you, nothing like you. But, oh, I love her. It doesn't mean I loved you any less. No one can replace you, Mandy. But Juliana's a delight. She's full of laughter and exuberance and song. She's impetuous and unpredictable.

Sometimes I wonder if I'll ever keep up with her. I'll never corral her spirit, but that's part of why I love her. She isn't you, Mandy. I knew you like I know my own soul, and I'll never forget you, darling. You taught me what love is all about, showed me how to open my heart and cherish a woman. Because of what you taught me about life and love, I believe I can make Juliana happy. Do I have your blessing, Mandy? I'd like to think I do.

Juliana's drowsy voice inquired, "Andrew? Are you okay?"

With a start he looked over at his wife. She had propped herself up on one elbow, her ebony hair cascading over her milky-white shoulders.

"Sure, I'm fine," he said, running his fingers over her arm. How could he confess to his lovely bride that he had been carrying on a mental conversation with his long-deceased wife?

"You looked so deep in thought. A million miles away."

"Yes, at least that," he conceded.

"Pleasant thoughts, I hope."

"Absolutely. What else on a sunny morning with my new bride beside me?" He reached over and gathered her into his arms. She nestled her head on his bare chest and he caught the scent of magnolias. How good she felt in his arms. He could hold her like this forever!

Being a man over the half-century mark in years, he hadn't expected to feel such a rush of what could only be described as youthful emotions. What a power there was in love. Falling in love was an indescribable intoxicant. With Juliana in his arms, he felt ageless, invincible; there was nothing he couldn't accomplish. He turned her lovely face up to his and kissed her soundly.

When she caught her breath, she murmured, "Andrew, dearest, what a wonderful way to start the day. Maybe we should skip breakfast and spend the entire morning —"

A determined knock on the door jarred them both.

"We're sleeping," Andrew called out, stifling his vexation.

"Not anymore!" The door eased open and Frannie peeked inside, her long blond hair flowing around her shoulders. She was wearing a tank top and cutoffs that showed off her golden tan. "Time for breakfast, you sleepyheads. It's almost nine, and you never go past 8:00 a.m., Daddy."

Andrew released Juliana, and she slipped down modestly under the covers.

Andrew cleared his throat uneasily and folded his arms over his bare chest. "We were thinking of skipping breakfast this morning, sweetheart."

"No, Daddy, it's not good for you to skip a meal. Besides, I have a surprise for your first morning home." Frannie breezed inside with a serving tray and set it on the bedside table.

As Andrew hoisted himself up, he caught the inviting aromas of bacon and coffee. "Honey, it smells wonderful, but —"

Juliana sat up, too, tucking the sheet around her shoulders. "Breakfast in bed? Oh, Frannie, you shouldn't have."

Frannie beamed. "It's nothing really. Just

bacon and eggs and cinnamon toast. Daddy's usual."

Juliana gave Frannie a stricken look. "Oh, dear, your father shouldn't be eating such things! Think of his cholesterol!"

Andrew reached for a slice of toast. "My cholesterol is fine and dandy, thank you."

Juliana lifted her chin truculently. "I don't care what you say, Andrew. A man your age should not be eating such fatty foods!"

"What do you mean, a man my age? What's wrong with my age?"

"Nothing is wrong with your age. But I intend to see that you live several more decades."

"By depriving me of bacon and eggs?"

Frannie snatched up the tray. "Listen, I could get you both something else. How about some cereal and yogurt?"

Juliana tossed back her waves of coal-black hair. "Thank you, Frannie. I will tell you the truth. I rarely eat breakfast. Maybe a little fruit now and then."

Frannie stepped back toward the door, her countenance darkening. "I'll remember that tomorrow, Juliana."

"Dear, please do not worry about your father and me. I will get our breakfast from now on. I am sure you have more important things to do."

"Nothing more important than taking care of my dad."

Andrew winced at the disappointment etched in his daughter's face. "We just don't want to put you out, honey."

"Your father is right. You work too hard. From now on I will fix breakfast."

"That's not necessary, Juliana. Daddy likes me to get his breakfast. Besides, I know just how he likes it."

Juliana flashed her most winsome smile. "But now it is time for me to learn."

Why did Andrew have the uneasy feeling he was witnessing a battle of wills, and he was the prize? With her trained voice and Italian accent, Juliana's words sounded almost lyrical. But Andrew could see them hitting Frannie like barbs. "You have had to take care of your father long enough, dear girl, and you have done a wonderful job. But you have your own life to live, and it's time your father let you live it."

"Wait a minute!" Andrew declared, raising his hands in a conciliatory, if not defensive, gesture. He could see trouble coming at him like a stampeding bull. "Hold on! Let's get this straight. I've never said Frannie couldn't live her own life. And I certainly never asked her to stay home and take care of me."

The misery in Frannie's eyes deepened. "You didn't have to ask, Daddy. I did it for Mother."

Andrew groaned. His awkward attempt to defuse the situation was igniting a firestorm too hot to handle. "Doll baby, your mom never would have expected you to sacrifice your life for me."

Frannie's big blue eyes clouded. "Sacrifice? Is that what you think I've been doing? Daddy, I thought you liked the way I took care of you!"

"I did, honey. I do! But I want so much more for you. Juliana's right. You need a life of your own."

Frannie balanced the tray and gripped the doorknob. Her lower lip quivered. "Don't beat around the bush. Just say it, Daddy! Now that you've got a new wife and daughter, I'm not needed around here anymore!"

Before Andrew could muster a reply, Frannie pivoted and marched out the door, slamming it so hard behind her, the walls rattled.

He threw back the covers and was about to go after his daughter, but Juliana stopped him and coaxed him back into bed. "You can't go after her dressed like that, Andrew. Let her be. She will get over it. We are a new family now. We all have adjustments to make. It will take time." She snuggled against his chest and he caught the delectable scent of her hair.

"Time?" he murmured, closing his eyes and inhaling deeply. That heady, intoxicating feeling was sweeping over him again. "My darling bride, do you suppose we have time for . . ." He let his words trail off as Juliana raised her face to his and kissed his lips with an ardor that left him breathless.

"My darling Andrew," she said in that throaty, beguiling voice of hers, "for you, there is always time!"

Chapter Two

Panic was growing inside Frannie like mushrooms in the dark. In June she had received a handsome commission to sculpt a bust of Longfellow for the La Jolla Children's Museum — due by the end of summer. It was already July, and all she could do was sit and stare at a mound of lifeless clay.

Try as she might, Frannie couldn't muster a shred of creativity. Her mind felt dry, numb, dead. She wondered if she had ever had a creative thought in her life. Had she ever experienced that flaming impulse to create something from nothing, or nearly nothing? Had she in the past actually molded fine sculptures — not masterpieces, of course, but still quality work — from heaps of wet, shapeless clay?

Where was the artist she had been just a few short weeks ago? How could her talent have fled so swiftly, so completely?

Every time she thought of sinking her fingers into that formless mass, she remembered something else she needed to do — some mindless chore or task that wouldn't usually demand her attention. With a sigh of resignation, she would drape the clay with a wet cloth, as if covering a dead body with a shroud. Then she would escape to another part of her house and fiddle with something, or busy herself in the kitchen, or stare out the window, or pester her father in his study — anything to keep from facing the task at hand, the challenge of pulling life and form out of that silent blob of gray earth.

Today held the same lack of promise. Right after breakfast, Frannie had gone to the sunroom to work. She had pored over a dozen drawings of the old poet and sketched several hurried renderings of her own. Then she had kneaded the clay until her fingers ached, until she admitted at last that she wasn't in the mood to create. God help her, she had lost her vision for the work.

Once, days or weeks ago, she had felt that creative impulse in her fingers, in her mind, in her heart. But now it was gone. An empty place remained, a vacuum, a hollow in her soul that nothing seemed to fill.

She had heard of writers and artists hitting

a dry spell, suffering writer's block and questioning their talent. But it hadn't happened to her. At least, not for several years. Not since . . . yes, she remembered now . . . not since her mother's death seven years ago.

For two years after her mother died, she hadn't been able to create a thing. She was seventeen at the time, fresh out of high school and just beginning her freshman year at San Diego State. Majoring in art, of course, as she had always planned. But every time she thought of creating something — a painting, a drawing, a vase or a piece of sculpture, she felt a knot of pain in her heart.

It was as if the idea of creation, even producing something as mundane as an object of art, signified a birth. The paradox was that her heart was deluged with the reality of death. But at last, praise God, when she began her junior year of college she experienced a breakthrough. Her creativity returned in a rush. She changed her major from art education to fine arts and completed her B.A. two years later.

And in the five years since then, her skill and reputation as a sculptor had grown. She was even teaching a night class at San Diego State . . . and the commissions were coming often enough that she had bankrolled a tidy sum in her savings account.

Yes, her life these days had been good, very good. Even though her evenings were devoid of romance, her routine had been satisfying and stable. . . . Until the last few weeks, when Frannie's world turned topsy-turvy — the day her father brought home his new bride and stepdaughter. Since then, nothing had been the same.

Take today, for example. In the past (B.J. — before Juliana), Frannie would have risen at seven and fixed her father's and Brianna's breakfast. The three of them would have sat around the table chatting about their plans for the day. They would have held hands and prayed together before going their separate ways.

But now that Brianna was married and setting up housekeeping in her own country estate, Frannie was lucky to see her once a week. And Cassie, with her new baby, stopped by even less often. Even when her sisters dropped in to visit, they chatted only about their happy new lives and then were quickly on their way. They were so busy and preoccupied, they were totally unaware that Frannie felt lonely and left behind.

It wasn't that the house was empty now. Frannie could have tolerated that. She had never minded long periods of solitude. The silence sometimes even stirred her creative juices. Peace and quiet were welcome friends.

But, in fact, the old Rowlands' homestead wasn't silent; it was as bustling as ever. It reverberated with noise and voices and music and laughter. But except for her father, the sounds belonged to strangers, not to the people Frannie loved.

In truth, even her father was different now. The dynamics had changed. He was a man absorbed with pleasing his wife. Where Frannie's happy home had once comfortably contained a father and three daughters, now her father was half of a newlywed couple occupying the premises. And each had a daughter. To complicate matters, Frannie and Belina were virtual strangers and had no desire to be anything more.

These days, Frannie's home was filled with Juliana's laughter and songs. In her youth, Juliana had performed on the New York stage and in the opera houses of Europe. Now her full, lilting soprano wafted through the Rowlands house a dozen times a day . . . as Juliana cooked and cleaned, as she taught voice lessons to eager children and led a women's Bible study twice a week in the parlor. Juliana was obviously determined to become the quintessential minister's wife — a fact Frannie resented.

But if Frannie begrudged the way Juliana had taken over her home, she was equally disturbed by the stealthy comings and goings of the mysterious Belina. The aloof, raven-haired girl was like a ghost, flitting through the house noiselessly, rarely speaking or making eye contact. She spent most of her time alone in her room doing who knew what.

Frannie was just as glad that she didn't have to make polite conversation with the strange young woman. What would they talk about? They had nothing in common . . . except that Belina's mother was married to Frannie's father.

Every morning, when Frannie awoke, she told herself, Maybe today things will be different. This will seem like my home again. I'll feel comfortable around Belina and Juliana. We'll begin to be a family at last.

But as quickly as she made her resolves, they were shattered by some minor event that caught Frannie unawares, that brought her up short and reminded her she was living in a vastly different household. It happened again today, the last week of July, just over two weeks since her father had brought Juliana home from their honeymoon.

This morning was the last straw for Frannie, because the incident involved someone dear to her heart. Ruggs, the family dog, an ancient, longhaired mongrel, had tracked mud all over Juliana's freshly waxed floor. Juliana chased him out the back door with a broom. Frannie had never seen the old dog run so fast or yelp so loud. The sound nearly broke Frannie's heart.

The problem was, Juliana just didn't get it. She considered Ruggs a scroungy old dog that was always getting in the way. She didn't understand that he was as much a member of the family as anyone. When Juliana shooed Ruggs out the door, it was as if she had shooed Frannie out, too.

Ten years ago, Brianna had found the scrawny, abandoned puppy on the street, hungry and shivering. She had brought him home and nursed him back to health, the way she nurtured everyone she came in contact with. And for ten years Ruggs had been king of the castle. There was no way Juliana was going to convince him he was just a mangy mutt.

The incident with Ruggs had left Frannie feeling more resentful of Juliana than ever. How dare that woman take over Frannie's home and chase her dog outside? The trouble was, these days Frannie felt as unwelcome as Ruggs in her own house. No wonder she wasn't in the mood to sculpt Longfellow's bust.

Even as she sat in the sunroom contemplating the mountain of clay on her worktable, Frannie could hear Juliana bustling about in the kitchen, crooning the lyrics from some Italian aria. Frannie worked with the clay for a few minutes, dipping her hands in a container of water and wetting down the gray mound. It still wasn't taking shape the way she wanted. It was as if the stubborn mass refused to relinquish the form hidden within.

Usually Frannie could work her artistic magic. A mysterious connection formed between her mind and hands; they worked together in a way Frannie herself couldn't comprehend. It was as if some secret force within her recognized the shape inside the mass and freed it, then she molded it until it came to life under her fingers.

That was the way it was supposed to work. But not today. In exasperation, Frannie pounded the clay with her fists, then tossed the wet cloth over it and went to the deep sink to wash her hands. If she couldn't sculpt anything worthwhile, she might as well go help Juliana in the kitchen. She emerged from the sunroom just as

Juliana hit a high note that rattled the crystal on the buffet.

Frannie ambled over to the kitchen sink where Juliana was scouring a black kettle, and said, "Looks like you could use some help."

Juliana whirled around and clasped her hand to her ample bosom. "Oh, dear girl, you startled me!"

"I'm sorry. I was going stir-crazy in the sunroom. The Longfellow bust — it's just not working for me."

"Oh, what a shame. Give it time, dear. It'll come." Juliana's rosy lips pursed together, forming a tiny rosebud of sympathy. She extended a graceful hand and touched Frannie's cheek with long, tapered fingers, her perfectly manicured nails a bright vermillion. "I have had many times when the music would not come, when I had to labor for every note. The arts do not give away their secrets easily. We must stretch and strain for every victory. But to create something beautiful is worth all the pain. It is like giving birth. Agony and ecstasy tied together. The agony of releasing something precious from within your secret self. And the ecstasy of holding in your hands a new life that only you and God could have created."

Frannie nodded distractedly. She wasn't

in the mood for a philosophical discussion about creativity.

Juliana set the kettle on the gas range, then reached for a can of tomatoes. Frannie's stomach knotted as she watched Juliana move about the kitchen as if she had already memorized — and claimed — every inch of it. She already considers it her private domain! Frannie noted grudgingly.

How could her father be so captivated by a woman like Juliana? The ebony-haired matron looked nothing like Frannie's idea of a minister's wife. Juliana was a buxom, brassy woman who made a habit of wearing colorful, formfitting dresses that were just short of being tacky. All right, so on Juliana they somehow managed to look classy in a dramatic, theatrical sort of way. That still didn't explain how her father could be so smitten by this flashy woman.

"What are you making?" Frannie asked as Juliana gathered an array of spices from the shelf.

Juliana paused and smiled at Frannie, her rosy face brightening. "I'm making spaghetti. Your father's favorite. We are entertaining his ministerial staff here tonight."

Frannie straightened, suddenly alert. "Tonight? They're coming for dinner? Why didn't Daddy tell me? He knows I teach my class tonight. There's no way I can fix spaghetti."

Juliana gently patted Frannie's arm. "No, dear girl, you don't understand. I will fix the spaghetti."

Frannie drew back from Juliana's touch. "But I always fix the spaghetti. Daddy won't be happy if I don't."

Juliana opened the cupboard and removed several cans of tomato sauce, then turned back to Frannie. "Well, we will straighten him out, won't we? We will tell him it's time for a change. I will fix my family's secret Italian recipe. I am sure your father will find it delightful."

Frannie wanted to retort, It won't be as good as mine! But she held her tongue. No sense in making waves. Her father would just take Juliana's side. "Well, let me know if you need any help."

"Thanks, dear. I'm fine." Juliana waved her ringed fingers in the air. "You go work on your sculpture."

A storm cloud of resentment swirled in Frannie's chest. Before she said something she regretted, Frannie strode back down the hall to the sunroom. As she looked back, she caught a glimpse of Belina slipping like a silent shadow into the kitchen. She was waiting for me to leave! The girl was so antisocial, she made every effort to avoid encounters with Frannie. What's her problem? Does she hate me? How can I live in the same house with someone who doesn't even want to look me in the eye or say good morning!

Frannie knew as soon as she sat down and gazed at the leaden mound of clay that she wasn't going to get any work done today. "Might as well take a drive and clear my head."

Frannie ran upstairs to her room and grabbed her purse off the bureau. On her way out the door she noticed Ruggs crouching on the floor by her bed. "Hey, boy, how did you get back in the house? Oh, I bet Daddy let you in, didn't he? While Juliana wasn't looking!"

Frannie knelt down and wrapped her arms around the rangy, mop-haired dog. He made a whining sound and ran his rough tongue over her arm. His shiny black eyes peered yearningly at her through several shanks of sandy-brown hair.

"Poor baby. Are you still smarting from your scolding this morning? Queen Juliana banished you from the kitchen, didn't she?" Frannie stood up, smoothed her jeans and beckoned the shaggy mongrel to follow her. "Come, boy. Let's go for a joyride!"

She scrambled down the stairs, with Ruggs bounding right behind her. She took long strides down the hall, peeked in her father's study and told him she was taking Ruggs for a ride to keep him out of Juliana's hair. Her father looked up from his sermon notes with a distracted smile and told her to have fun.

"Sure, Daddy. See you later." She sighed dispiritedly as she headed out the door. *He doesn't have a clue how miserable I am since he married Juliana! Not a clue!*

Outside, in the driveway, Frannie opened the passenger door of her shiny yellow sports car and coaxed Ruggs inside. "Sit still now and be a good boy."

Out on the open road, she looked over at Ruggs and grinned. Her hirsute pet sat tall, panting happily as the warm breeze rolled through the open window and fanned his heavy fur.

"Let's go to the ocean and be beach bums for a day," she suggested, as if expecting a reply. Ruggs accommodated her with an agreeable yip.

She took La Jolla Shores Drive for several miles, then turned off on a small winding road that led to a lonely expanse of beach. She parked beside the road, let Ruggs out and the two ambled across the sand under a shimmering white-hot sun. At the water's edge, she pulled off her sandals, rolled up her pant legs and waded barefoot into the cool water. Ruggs started to follow, then backed up as a wave rippled over his paws.

Frannie laughed. "Oh, come on, you chicken. Come in the water! You won't melt."

Ruggs took another lumbering step backward and shook himself. No dip in the sea for him. He was staying high and dry.

As if to defy her stubborn pet, Frannie waded out deeper. A ringlet of seaweed caught her ankle. She kicked it away and noticed a creamy white shell in the water. She stooped down, picked it up and brushed off the wet sand. It was a perfect shell. She breathed in the fresh, briny air, filling her lungs. There was something she loved about the beach. A sense of freedom and adventure, as if the world were wide open, boundless, offering endless possibilities. And yet, somehow, standing there, she could stretch out her arms and touch the earth from end to end.

"I could stay here forever," she told Ruggs. "I feel like I could sit down right here and sink my hands in the wet sand and create something beautiful."

Ruggs ignored her and pawed at something

slimy on the hard-packed sand. Frannie chose not to look too closely. "Come on, Ruggsy," she urged. "Let's explore!"

She slogged a while through the ankle-deep water, then made her way up the beach and padded across the warm, uneven sand. They had walked a quarter mile when Frannie spotted an old clapboard beach house nestled beside a rocky protuberance. Jutting cliffs dotted with palm trees rose beyond the modest little house. The place looked empty, its door padlocked. A weathered sign stood at an angle beside the house. It said For Rent. Call 555-7878.

Frannie shaded her eyes and gazed into the distance along the isolated beach. There were other houses, but they were far and few between. Anyone living in this house would have complete privacy, not to mention peace and quiet.

"This is just what we need, Ruggs. A place to call our own, with no one to disturb us. What do you say, boy? Shall we check it out?"

Ruggs galumphed toward the house. Frannie caught up with him as he clambered onto the small wood-frame porch and pawed the warped pine door. Frannie rubbed a layer of dirt off the window and peered inside. To her surprise, the little house was furnished. To be sure, the modest furnishings looked a bit dilapidated, but comfortable.

"Wouldn't it be a hoot to move into this place? What do you think, Ruggs?" she asked, as if the pooch might actually respond.

He backed up and let out an approving howl. At least, that's how she chose to interpret it.

"So you like it, too, boy. It's something to think about." She memorized the phone number and gave the house another once-over, then she and Ruggs headed back down the beach to her car.

Until now she had never seriously considered moving out of her father's house. As long as he had needed her, she had vowed to be there for him. But the bitter truth was, he didn't need her anymore. He had Juliana and her strange, reclusive daughter, and he seemed perfectly content to make them his family now.

But maybe her father's marriage was a blessing in disguise. Frannie was twenty-four now, too old to still be living at home under her daddy's watchful eye. Maybe it was time to step out, explore the world and carve a new life for herself. There was no telling what — or who — awaited her in this vast, beckoning land.

Chapter Three

For two days, Frannie put off phoning the rental number to inquire about the beach house. She vacillated between excitement at the prospect of moving into a place of her own and horror at the thought of leaving her father and the home she had lived in all her life. Wouldn't moving out show that she had truly given up on salvaging her family? Or was God trying to tell her something, nudging her to take responsibility for her own life and future?

On the third day, Frannie gathered her courage and dialed the number. She learned the house was still available and the rent was less than she might have expected for beach-front property, even though the house was a bit dilapidated. "I'll take it," she heard herself saying. Her heart began to pound with anticipation and a pinch of anxiety.

What am I doing? she asked herself the

next day as she drove to the beach house to meet the real estate agent for an official walk-through. “What could I have been thinking?” she wondered aloud an hour later as she returned home with a signed rental agreement and a set of keys.

That evening she cornered her father in his study and told him the news. By the stunned look on his face, she might as well have told him she was taking the next shuttle into space.

“Aren’t you happy here, sugar plum?” he asked blankly.

She fought the tears gathering in her eyes. She couldn’t — wouldn’t — lose control. All she could manage to blurt out was “You have Juliana now, and you like her spaghetti better than mine!”

He got up from his desk, came around and drew her into his arms. “Spaghetti? This is about spaghetti?”

“No, Daddy. It’s just . . . you don’t need me anymore. You have a new family.”

He caressed her hair. “I’ll always need you, baby cakes. You know that. I need you to be my loving daughter, but not my cook, housekeeper and caretaker. I let you fill those roles much too long.” He kissed her forehead. “And who says I like Juliana’s spaghetti better than yours? Nothing can top yours.”

Frannie sniffled like a sulking child. "You're not just saying that?"

Her father grinned broadly. "Are you kidding? I'm a minister of the Gospel. I'm committed to telling the truth, and only the truth. And the truth is, I saw this coming. I understand why you'd want a place of your own. But I'll miss you like crazy, pumpkin. And no matter where you go or what you do, nobody can take your place in my heart."

She smiled through her tears. "Then I have your blessing?"

"My blessing, my love and my prayers. I just ask you to make sure this is what you really want. And promise me, anytime you decide this isn't for you, you'll come home."

"Don't worry. I'll come home to visit. I'll be here so often, you'll get sick of me."

"Never in a million years." Her father kissed her forehead, then clasped her face in his large hands. "This beach house — is it safe? In a good area?"

"Of course, Daddy. It's perfect."

"Well, I have an idea. Why don't you take Ruggs with you? I'd feel better knowing he's there to protect you."

"You wouldn't mind?"

Her father winked. "Juliana's not too fond of the old boy anyway. You take him."

Frannie threw her arms around her father's neck. "Thank you, Daddy! Thank you!"

She turned to leave, but he caught her hand. "You know, there's someone else who's going to miss you. Now Belina won't have anyone in the house her age to hang out with."

Frannie rolled her eyes. Was it possible her father really didn't have a clue about Belina? "Daddy, she'll be very happy to have me out of here. You just wait and see."

"I don't believe that for a minute. I think she'd like the two of you to be friends."

"Then she can come visit me at my beach house." Fat chance that would ever happen!

Her father seemed to think that was a good idea. "I'll tell her that. She used to live on the beach. I bet she misses it."

"Whatever," Frannie mumbled. Spooky Belina was the last person she wanted hanging out at her new place, but she couldn't tell her father that.

The next afternoon, after lunch, her father helped her carry her things out to the car. She wasn't taking much — some clothes, toiletries, her Bible, CD player, boombox and enough dishes, pots and pans and utensils to accommodate one person. On the weekend her father and Juliana's son, Antonio, would rent a truck and bring out all her art supplies and equipment from the sunroom.

"Are you sure you don't want me to come with you today?" her father asked as she coaxed Ruggs into the passenger seat. "I could help you settle in. The place might need some work. I could get my toolbox and —"

"No, Daddy, you stay here. I'm fine. I've got to do this myself. I'm grown up, Dad. I'm not Daddy's little girl anymore." She didn't add that she feared her father would have a fit if he saw how desolate and in disrepair the beach house was. She could hear him now. I won't have my daughter living in a hovel like this! And look how isolated you are! It's not safe. What if someone breaks in — ?

No, she didn't want him seeing her new home until she'd had a chance to settle in and spruce it up a bit. Once she had all her things in place, her father would be reluctant to insist she move out and come home.

It was late afternoon before Frannie pulled her vehicle into the small, rutted driveway beside her new home. Her heart was pounding with excitement as she slipped out of her car, let Ruggs out and walked across the beach to the modest dwelling. "Well, here we are, Ruggsy. Home at last!" She stuck the key in the lock and turned it, then gingerly opened the door. It creaked on its hinges. She made a mental note: Oil the hinges. She stepped inside and gazed around at her very own domicile.

The thought came to her: Be it ever so humble, there's no place like home. Her gaze flitted over the hardwood floor, the paneled walls, braided throw rugs, pine tables with hurricane lamps and several pieces of overstuffed furniture, worn and sagging, but adequate. Besides the small bedroom and bath down the narrow hallway, the house consisted of one large room, with a breakfast bar separating the kitchen from the living area and a rustic stone fireplace taking up most of one wall.

Frannie sank down on the lumpy couch and bounced gently, testing the springs. "Well, they're right about the humble part. It's not Beverly Hills. But we'll get along just fine, won't we, Ruggsy?"

Ruggs loped around the room, sniffing every corner, then settled on the braided rug at Frannie's feet. She reached down and massaged his floppy ears. "We can't sit around loafing all day, Ruggs. We've got work to do." She riffled through her purse and found her cell phone. "I'd better call the phone company and see when they can start service. Can't depend on my cell phone forever." She punched in the numbers and waited, then tossed the phone back in her purse. "Might know. In all my excitement, I forgot to charge the battery last night. We're off to a good start, aren't we!"

She got up and went to her kitchenette and turned on the spigot. The pipes groaned and clattered. Rusty water finally sputtered from the faucet. "Doesn't look like this place has been occupied in ages." She opened the cupboards. They would need to be washed out and lined before she stocked them. "Looks like I'd better bring in my stuff and find the detergent."

It took several trips to unload her car. She couldn't believe she had packed so much. And wait till her father came with the rest of her stuff on Saturday! Now that she had boxes, sacks and suitcases everywhere, the place looked smaller than ever. And a bit grungy, if she was honest about it. No second thoughts! she warned herself. You wanted a place of your own, and now you've got it. Make the best of it!

For the next hour she scrubbed the kitchen cupboards. While they weren't exactly gleaming, they finally looked tolerable.

"I'm done! They'll have to do." Wiping her chapped hands on a paper towel, she looked over at Ruggs, ensconced by the stone fireplace. "Guess I'd better make a trip to the grocery store, or we'll be having stale granola bars and rusty water for dinner. You stay here, boy, and keep an eye on the place, and I'll bring you back your favorite doggie treats."

Ruggs barked and wagged his tail.

Frannie grabbed up her purse, checked for her keys and retraced her steps across the sandy yard to her car. The air had cooled perceptibly and clouds were gathering on the horizon. "You might know," she mumbled as she pulled out onto the street. "My first day in my new house and it looks like rain. It hardly ever rains in Southern California in July! Hope I'm not stuck with a leaky roof."

The closest grocery store was a small market several miles away. Hope I don't see anybody I know, she thought as she entered the store. She was wearing formfitting jeans and a white blouse tied at her waist, and her long blond hair looked unattended and flyaway in the rising breeze. Seeing that the store was nearly empty, she gave a little sigh of relief. Thank goodness, she wouldn't be encountering any prospective dates in a place like this.

She bought just enough staples to tide her over for the next few days — two paper sacks filled with milk, butter, bread, eggs, oatmeal, ground beef, salad fixings and a healthy selection of fresh fruits and vegetables. She remembered Ruggs's dog food and treats and even snuck in a bag of chips and munchies for herself, plus a six-pack of diet cola. At the checkout counter, she added a local newspaper, a nice way to keep in touch with the world, since she had decided not to bring a television set.

By the time she returned to the beach house, the clouds had swollen to a threatening black and the wind was rattling the shutters, as if demanding entrance. Balancing her two bags of groceries, Frannie got inside just as the wind banged the door shut behind her.

"Wow! Looks like we're in for quite a storm."

Ruggs gazed up at her and cocked his head in agreement. She gave him a treat, then put the groceries away. She hadn't noticed before how old and small the refrigerator was. She hoped it worked. Why hadn't she been more careful to check things when she'd had her walk-through?

A sudden pelting rain slammed against

the roof and rattled the windows. She looked outside and groaned. It was a downpour. The thought occurred to her to go back home just for tonight to get out of this storm. She immediately dismissed the idea. How would it look for her to go hightailing it home her very first day?

She shivered and realized she had no idea how to heat the place. She scrutinized the fireplace. Sure, why not? This was her home now. If she wanted to have a little fire in her own fireplace, who was to stop her? She stooped down beside the hearth and moved the grate aside. To her surprise, it already held several charred logs. Now if she could just find the matches she had packed in one of the boxes.

By the time she located the matches, it was dark outside and the rain was coming down harder than ever. A bone-chilling dampness seeped through the walls, one of the disadvantages of living in a bungalow perched on the edge of the ocean.

Frannie bent over the fireplace and made sure the flue was open, then took the classified section from the paper, lit it and coaxed the flames until they ignited the blackened wood. After several minutes she had a roaring fire. Frannie stepped back and folded her arms in satisfaction. See, she was a smart, capable, independent woman. She could manage without her father's help!

Feeling a hunger pang or two, she returned to the kitchen and browsed through her groceries. Time for dinner. Maybe she would fix a salad, some broccoli and a hamburger. Not a feast exactly, but certainly adequate.

As she broke open a head of lettuce, she smelled something burning. How could that be? She hadn't turned on the gas range. A crackling noise broke into the distant drumming of the rainfall. Ruggs barked. Frannie spun around and gazed across the room, the lettuce dropping from her fingers. Heavy, black smoke was billowing out of the fireplace and filling the house.

Frannie ran to the fireplace and grabbed the poker. If she could only smother the flames! But her awkward attempts were useless. The flames were too intense and the smoke too thick. Her eyes started smarting, her throat went dry and she began to cough. She couldn't see. The acrid fumes were already stealing her breath. She dashed to the bedroom for her cell phone, then remembered that the battery was dead. She ran back to the living room and stared helplessly at the rolling smoke blanketing the room.

With her heart pounding in her throat,

she grabbed Ruggs by the collar. "Come on, boy! Gotta find a phone and call the fire department!"

The moment she and Ruggs stepped out on the porch, she knew her trouble had only begun. The rain was coming down in a blinding deluge. There was no way she could drive.

"Dear God, help us!" She looked around, the rain streaming down her face and soaking her clothes. The world was a mass of liquid shadows and elusive shapes. Then, through the leaden gloom she saw a light flickering in the distance. It was the cottage down the beach. Someone was home!

"Come on, Ruggs!" Frannie broke into a run, her sneakers filling with water, her wet clothes sticking to her skin. She was drenched and out of breath by the time she reached the bungalow. She scaled the porch steps and pounded on the door until her palms ached. It seemed like an eternity before the latch clicked and the door creaked open.

Frannie caught a glimpse of a towering silhouette in the doorway, etched against the rosy glow of lamplight inside.

"I need a phone," she blurted.

"Don't have one."

"Please! My house is on fire!"

The man stepped outside. He was tall and brawny, his face obscured by shadows. "Where?"

She pointed down the beach. "There! The next cabin!"

The man pushed past her and broke into a sprint. She nudged Ruggs and ran after him, her legs suddenly feeling like overcooked spaghetti. She slipped in a puddle and nearly went down. Somehow she caught herself and slogged on through the relentless torrents. She arrived at the beach house just as the man disappeared inside. She clambered onto the porch and pushed open the door. Smoke rolled over her.

Inside, the man's deep, rasping voice bellowed, "Get out!"

She backed away, letting the door bang shut, and waited, holding Ruggs by the collar as the rain pelted them mercilessly. What if the stranger died trying to salvage her cabin? He could be asphyxiated by the fumes. How long did she dare wait before entering the house again?

Her questions were answered moments later, when the man burst out the door, his brawny chest heaving as he sucked for air. He was covered with soot, the stench of charred kindling so pungent on his body that Frannie turned her face away.

He took her arm and urged her away from the cabin. "Come on!"

She dug in her heels. "No — my house!"

"It's okay. I smothered the fire. Nothing's burning!"

"But I can't just leave it."

He stared down at her, impatience etched in his blackened face. "You can't stay, lady. It's toxic in there. We'll air it out tomorrow."

He took her hand and pulled her after him as if she were an obstreperous child. "Let's go!"

She stumbled after him. "Where?"

"My place, unless you've got a better idea."

She followed numbly, Ruggs galumphing after them through the downpour. By the time they reached the man's bungalow, Frannie's teeth were chattering. He opened the door and stepped aside. She hesitated only a moment as she recalled from childhood her mother's repeated admonition *Never go in the house of strangers.* This time there seemed no other choice. Besides, she had Ruggs. He would protect her, unless the man made him stay outside.

She sighed with relief when he held the door for Ruggs, too. After Ruggs bounded inside and shook himself like an oversize mop, spraying water everywhere, the man came in and shut the door behind him. He broke into a spasm of coughing.

She looked at him with concern. "The fumes got to you."

He wiped his red-rimmed eyes. "I'm okay." He pulled a handkerchief from the pocket of his jeans and coughed into it.

Frannie politely looked away. Folding her arms to keep from shivering, she gazed around the cottage and realized how good it felt to be inside a nice, warm house. The furnishings were as spartan as those in her cabin — masculine pine furniture, worn overstuffed couch and chair, hurricane lamps, braided rugs and a red brick fireplace with a crackling fire. The cottage was nothing fancy, but at the moment it seemed immensely inviting.

The man touched her arm, and she jumped. "You'd better get out of those clothes, miss."

She shrank back, her heart pounding. What if this stranger was a homicidal maniac? He was well over six feet tall and close to two hundred pounds. She'd be helpless to fight him off.

"I'm f-fine," she stammered.

"No, you're not. You'll freeze in those wet clothes."

She slipped over by the fire and held out her hands. "I'll just warm up a minute and then be on my way."

The man guffawed. "Really? You'll be on your way . . . where?"

"Home." They were both in this miserable predicament, and he was laughing at her! "I'll dry off, then go back to my house. The smoke should be tolerable by then."

Even with his face smudged with soot and his eyes tearing, the man managed a twinkle of amusement. "You're not getting rid of that smoke until you open all the doors and windows and air the place out in the heat of day."

Frannie's ire rose. She didn't want anyone telling her something that she wasn't ready to accept — the fact that she was stuck in a strange house with a strange man for the duration of a bleak, rainy night. "I won't be here long," she insisted. "Once I've dried off, I'll go get my car and drive to my father's house."

"You'd have to be a fool to drive in this deluge."

"Well, I certainly can't stay here all night."

"Have it your way." He pulled his wet T-shirt over his head.

Frannie gasped. "What are you doing?"

"I'm going to go take a shower and see if I can scrub off some of this grime. And make the fire stop burning in my eyes."

As he rolled his blackened shirt in a ball, Frannie couldn't help noticing that he had the muscular build of a football player or weight lifter. He started down the hallway, then paused and looked back at her. "Listen, I've got some clothes you can change into, or a blanket —"

"No, I'm o-okay."

"That's why your teeth are chattering so hard you can't talk?"

He was right. She was freezing inside and out. If she didn't get out of these wet clothes, she'd catch her death of cold. "Maybe . . . maybe I will change."

He grinned, showing white, even teeth in his smudged face. "Fine. I'll lay some things out in the bedroom and you can change in there. There's a lock on the door, if you're worried. I'll be in the bathroom showering."

It sounded reasonable enough. Maybe the guy was harmless. She nodded. "I'd appreciate some warm clothes."

He disappeared down the hall, then returned a minute later and led her to the bedroom. "My things are way too big for you. But I found a flannel shirt and some sweats with a drawstring, so they should stay up okay. If you're still cold, you can wrap yourself in a blanket. Just take one off the bed."

"Thank you." She was still hugging herself, shivering. As soon as he stepped out of the room, she shut the door and bolted the lock. After removing her soggy sneakers, she quickly peeled off her soaked jeans and blouse and hung them over the metal bedpost. Her underwear was damp, but she wasn't about to part with it. She pulled on the long-sleeve shirt and baggy sweats and pulled the strings until they were cinched around her narrow waist.

For the first time she glanced at herself in the bureau mirror and shuddered. Who was this straggly, ragamuffin waif looking back at her with smeared makeup and disheveled hair? She looked like something out of a fright movie. Oh, well, the last thing on her mind was impressing anybody, especially her churlish stranger.

Gingerly she unlocked the door and peered down the hall. No one in sight. She heard the shower running in the bathroom. And — was it possible? — a deep voice was crooning a country-western song. The nerve of that man, to be singing so nonchalantly when they were in such a dire predicament!

She pulled a blanket off the bed, wrapped

it around her shoulders and tiptoed down the hall past the bathroom. When she heard the shower go off, she scurried on to the living room and curled up on the couch before the fireplace — a little bug in a rug, as her mom used to say.

The man's voice sounded from the hallway. "You through in the bedroom, miss?"

"Yes, it's all yours," she called back, quelling a fresh spurt of anxiety. Now what? Was she actually going to spend an entire night in this house? Was she safe?

After a few minutes, the man came striding into the living room in a fresh T-shirt and jeans. He was toweling his dark, curly hair. His eyes were still tearing. But without all the soot and grime, he looked uncommonly handsome. His strong classic features were as finely chiseled as a Michelangelo sculpture — a perfectly straight nose, high forehead and sharply honed cheekbones, a wide jaw and a full, generous mouth. Arched brows shaded intense brown eyes and the stubble of a beard shadowed his chin.

Frannie realized she was staring.

He tossed his towel over a chair and eyed her suspiciously. "Is there a problem, lady?"

Frannie felt her face grow warm. "No,

I'm sorry. I was concerned about your eyes. I hope the smoke didn't hurt them."

"They smart a little, but they'll be okay." He sat down in the overstuffed chair and raked his damp hair back from his forehead. "What I want to know is how you got all that smoke backed up in your house like that."

Frannie tightened the blanket around her shoulders. "I just started a fire, that's all. How did I know it was going to back up into the house?" She tossed him a defensive glance. "I checked the flue, if that's what you're wondering."

He sat forward and held his hands out to the lapping flames. "But did you check the chimney to make sure some bird hadn't built a nest in it? Or the winds hadn't stuffed it with debris? No telling how long it's been since someone built a fire in that place."

Frannie shook her head. "I didn't think of that."

"Next time, get yourself a chimney sweep before you go starting a fire."

She bristled. "I will. First thing tomorrow. Or . . . whenever the rain stops."

He coughed again, a dry, hacking sound that shook his hefty frame.

"You inhaled too much smoke. Maybe you should see a doctor."

He laughed, and coughed again. "No way

to see a doctor tonight. Maybe I'll fix a little tea and lemon. Want some?"

She shivered in spite of the dry clothes and heavy blanket. "Yes, some hot tea would be wonderful."

He stood and gazed down at her. "Listen, neighbor, if we're going to spend the night together, there's something you need to know."

She gazed up at him with a start, her backbone tensing. The rain was still hammering the roof, its relentless rat-a-tat echoing the fierce pounding of her heart. "Something I should know? What's that?"

He held out his hand. "My name. I'm Scott. Scott Winslow. What's yours?"

She relaxed a little and allowed a flicker of a smile to cross her lips. "I — I'm Frannie. Frannie Rowlands." She slipped her hand out of the blanket and allowed his large, rough hand to close around it.

He matched her smile. "Well, Frannie, it's going to be a long night. We might as well make the best of it."

Chapter Four

Frannie was on her guard again. She tightened her grip on the blanket wrapped around her, then glanced over at Ruggs curled contentedly beside the fireplace. If Scott Winslow tried anything suspicious, surely Ruggs would come to her defense. Wouldn't he? Or would he just roll over and go to sleep and leave her to fend for herself?

"Sugar and cream?"

"What?"

"Your tea. Do you want it plain? With lemon? Or with sugar and cream?" A faint smile played on the man's lips, but his eyes held a hint of something darker. Was it despair, nostalgia, remorse? "My mother was an Englishwoman. She always had a spot of cream in her tea."

"Plain is fine for me. Just as long as it's hot."

While he fixed the tea, Frannie gazed

around the room, assessing what sort of man she was keeping company with tonight. *Please, dear Lord, don't let him be an ax murderer!* There wasn't much to go on — a few books on a table, a radio on the counter. But no television, stereo or telephone. Nor were there any newspapers, magazines, knick-knacks or family portraits in sight. And not even a calendar or a cheap print on the wall.

Who is this man? Frannie wondered. He's anonymous. There's nothing in this room that tells me who he is. Except perhaps his books.

She reached out from her blanket for the nearest book and turned it over in her hands. It looked like a library book, some sort of historical treatise. Did the man possess nothing of his own? As she put it back, she noticed an open Bible lying among the history books, philosophy tomes and suspense novels.

A man who reads the Bible can't be all bad, she mused.

As Scott served the tea, she let the blanket fall away from her shoulders and accepted the steaming mug. With the tea warming her insides, her flannel shirt and sweats should be enough to keep her toasty. She put the mug to her lips and sipped gingerly, then nodded toward the stack of books.

"You must like to read."

He settled back in his overstuffed chair and took a swallow of the hot liquid. "Yes, I do. It's one of my favorite pastimes."

"Mine, too. When I have time."

He flashed an oblique smile. "I always have time."

"You're lucky. I'm always juggling a busy schedule."

"And mine is wide open these days."

She ventured another observation. "I see you have a Bible."

He nodded. "It was my mother's."

"Was?"

"Yes." He paused, as if deliberating whether to go on. Finally he said in a low, abrupt voice, "She — she died."

Frannie felt a jolt of emotions — sympathy, empathy, compassion and her own lingering pain. "I'm sorry."

"Don't be. It's been a while."

"How long?"

"Well over six months."

Frannie turned the warm mug in her palms. "My mother died seven years ago, and I still can't believe she's gone."

Scott looked away, but not before Frannie saw tears glistening in his eyes. His voice rumbled. "Seven years? Then it sounds like I've got a long way to go."

Frannie searched for words. "Scott, I hope your mother's Bible has been a comfort for you."

"I'm trying to find in it what she found."

"I'm sure she'd be pleased that you kept it."

His eyes darkened. "It's the least I could do." He leaned forward and set his mug on the table, then folded his hands under his chin. His brows furrowed and the lines around his mouth deepened as he gazed at the flames. He was a young man, surely no more than thirty, but the heaviness in his expression made him look old beyond his years.

Frannie had the feeling he was debating whether or not to say more, perhaps even to open up to her about his feelings. She took the initiative. "Losing someone you love . . . There are no words for it. But it does help to talk about it, even when you don't know what to say."

His voice was noncommittal. "I suppose you're right."

"And sometimes talking to a stranger is easier than baring your soul to your loved ones."

He nodded. "Ironic, but true."

"When my mother died, I didn't talk about my feelings for a long time. I was afraid my father and sisters would feel worse if they knew how much I was hurting."

Scott gave her a probing, incisive glance. "Then how did you cope?"

She gazed at the flickering fire for several moments. "I don't know. I'm not even sure what coping means. I just tried to make it through each day. I prayed a lot. Cried a lot. Ranted a little." She held up the thumb-worn Bible. "And I looked for answers in this book."

His lips tightened in a small, ironic smile. "So we have something in common. Two motherless orphans with a penchant for the Holy Scriptures. Extraordinary."

"Not really. I've read the Bible all my life. You might say I was spoon-fed from the cradle."

"How so?"

"My father's a minister."

He looked at her curiously, one brow arching. "Is that so? What's it like?"

"Being a minister's daughter?" She chuckled. "Don't get me going on that subject."

"Why not? The rain's not letting up. We've got a long night ahead of us."

Frannie shivered and pulled the blanket back up around her shoulders. He was right. The uncertainty of her situation struck her afresh. She didn't know the first thing about this man. She might have stepped heedlessly into her worst nightmare. She would have to endure an entire night to find out. She drummed her fingers on the mug. "I really need to let my father know where I am. He's such a worrywart. He might even come looking for me."

"He'd be crazy to go out in this weather."

It was true. Her father wouldn't be looking for her. He had no idea she even needed him. Frannie sipped her tea. It was lukewarm now. She glanced at her watch. She had been here for nearly two hours. She was cold and exhausted. All she wanted was to be back in her father's house, in her own bed, safe and sound.

But there was something in the remote, melancholy face of the man sitting in the chair beside her that touched her and piqued her curiosity. Staring morosely into the fire, he looked like the loneliest man in the world. Or maybe that's the way he wanted it . . . To be alone. He hadn't anticipated that he would have to rescue a damsel in distress and take her back to his cottage for the night.

Frannie shifted uneasily on the couch. She drew her legs up under her and tucked the blanket around her knees. Rain still pelted the roof and windows like an invisible intruder, demanding admittance. She cleared her throat and waited to see if her moody companion would break the silence. The rosy glow from the flames danced on his stalwart features, but he remained tight-lipped, stony-faced.

Finally she spoke his name, startling him out of his reverie. "Mr. Winslow?"

He stared at her as if he had forgotten she was there. "Did you say something?"

"Just your name."

"I'm sorry. My mind wandered. I guess I'm guilty of that a lot these days."

"No problem. It took me a year after my mother died before I could concentrate on anything again. People talked to me and I never heard a word. I'd try to work and end up staring at a shapeless mound of clay all day."

Bewilderment flickered in his eyes. "You stared at a mound of clay? I've heard of many ways to express grief, but that's a new one on me."

Frannie broke into laughter. Scott joined her with a polite, baffled chuckle, but she knew he had no idea what was so funny. She covered her mouth to stifle herself. "I'm sorry. There's no way you could know. I'm a sculptor. The clay had nothing to do with grieving. It's my job. What I do."

He grinned sheepishly. "Now I get it. I'm impressed. I've never met a sculptor before."

She smiled. "Most people look at me with suspicion or pity. They figure I'm in my second childhood or never got out of my first. They can't imagine a grown woman mucking around in clay all day."

"Good training for a muddy night like this."

"I suppose so."

"And you're doing what you love best."

She arched her brows, wide-eyed. "How do you know that?"

He grinned. "I see it in your face. Hear it in your voice. You're obviously passionate about your work."

"I didn't realize it showed."

"Like neon lights."

She felt a warm glow that had nothing to do with the fire. "So what do you do?"

He didn't answer for a full minute. She was about to repeat the question in case he had reverted back into his reverie. But finally he spoke. "What do I do? I walk. I run. I collect driftwood on the beach. I read. I think. Sometimes I even try to pray."

"Sounds like a very peaceful life. But I meant, what kind of work do you do?"

"I just told you."

She laughed lightly. "You know what I mean. I assume you have a job to go to. You're too young to be retired. Oh, I know. You're on vacation. Renting this cabin for the summer."

He shook his head, his expression clouding, as if he were deliberately stepping back behind a veil. "This isn't a summer cottage. It's my permanent home."

Frannie ran her fingertips over the scratchy blanket that enveloped her. "I'm sorry. I didn't mean to sound nosy. It's none of my business what line of work you're in."

Scott got up and stoked the fire, then sat back down. "I'm not trying to be evasive, Miss Rowlands. The truth is, this is what I do. This is it. I live in this cottage. Sometimes I collect and sell firewood."

Disappointment scissored through Frannie. She had imagined that her handsome rescuer might be a doctor, lawyer or business tycoon. Surely anything but a common beach bum.

"When I'm in the mood, I build furniture out of driftwood, but it's not a profitable occupation. It takes me too long to create each piece, and no one's willing to meet my price."

"I know the feeling," Frannie conceded.

"Sculpting is like that at times. It's feast or famine. When I have a commission I'm on easy street. When I don't, I'm on a penny-pincher's budget. It was never a problem when I lived at home, but now that I'm on my own . . ."

"It can be a challenge," he agreed. "But I always have a few dollars in my pocket. Enough to get by."

"Did you ever think of, um, you know, going out and —"

"Getting a real job?"

"Something like that."

Scott's voice took on an oddly menacing tone, as if he were lashing out at some invisible adversary. "The corporate world is filled with potholes and booby traps. I've seen men swallowed whole by the duplicity and hypocrisy. I've seen them sell their souls and the souls of their families for just a little more power and wealth. It's a deadly, diabolic life. I want no part of it."

There was only the sound of the thundering downpour until Frannie found her voice. "It doesn't have to be that way, Mr. Winslow. I've known some very honorable businessmen. Men who are honest and generous and —"

He stood abruptly. "It's late, Miss Rowlands." He took a step toward her, his towering frame silhouetted against the fire-light. "I imagine you'd like to get some sleep."

A knot of apprehension tightened in Frannie's chest as he loomed over her. "Sleep? I — I hadn't thought about it."

"It's nearly midnight."

She shrank back against the couch, her fingers clutching the blanket around her shoulders. What would she do if this strange, agitated man attacked her? Ruggs, asleep by the fire, couldn't save her. And there wasn't another living soul in shouting distance. She might be able to grab the poker, knock him out and run. But where would she go in this deluge? And surely with his strength, he could wrestle the poker from her grip and use it on her.

Her fear crescendoed as he held out his hand and said in a tone both forceful and compelling, "Come, Miss Rowlands. Don't be afraid. You know where the bedroom is."

Chapter Five

"I don't need the bedroom, Mr. Winslow. I'm fine right here on the couch," Frannie declared with all the boldness she could muster.

"Nonsense, Miss Rowlands. You're my guest. You take the bedroom and I'll take the couch. It's the least I can do."

"All right, if you insist."

"I insist."

Relief washed over her. Thank heavens, he meant her no harm. He was just offering her a place to sleep! Still wrapped in her blanket, she got up off the couch and headed for the bedroom. She recalled the lock on the door. It meant she could rest without fear.

But when Scott followed her down the hall into the bedroom, her anxieties sparked again. He went over to the bed and pulled off a blanket. Then, seeing the expression on her face, he held up his palm in a gesture of peace. "Don't worry, I'm just getting myself a blanket." He looked back at the bed. "I could change the sheets if you want to wait a minute."

Frannie waved him off. "No, thanks, I'll probably just curl up on top of the bed."

"Well, make yourself at home. You're the first company I've had here. It's nothing fancy, but I think you should be comfortable. I'll put clean towels in the bathroom. Feel free to shower if you like."

Frannie took a backward step and shook her head. "I'm pretty tired. I'll just get some shut-eye."

"Fine. Mind if I take one of the pillows?"

"Of course. They're yours."

Scott grabbed a pillow and tucked it under his arm with the blanket. He stood beside the bed for a moment, gazing at Frannie. In the soft glow of the hurricane lamp, he looked ruggedly handsome. "So I guess we're all set, Miss Rowlands. Sleep well. I'll see you in the morning."

"Yes. Thank you. Good night." As he started for the door, she said, "Wait! I forgot about Ruggs. I should bring him in here with me."

Scott looked back at her and shrugged. "He's fine sleeping by the fire. I doubt you'll be able to rouse him anyway."

"I know, but I just thought —"

Comprehension flickered in his eyes. "Oh, you think you'll be safer with your dog in here with you. Is that it?"

"I — I didn't say that."

"But I can see it in your eyes. What do you think I'll do, Miss Rowlands? Attack you in my own home? I assure you, you have nothing to fear from me."

Her cheeks warmed with embarrassment. "I didn't mean to offend you, Mr. Winslow. But you must admit we find ourselves in a rather unusual situation."

"Circumstances always look worse in the midst of a howling storm. Don't worry. Things will look infinitely better in the morning. Good night again, Miss Rowlands."

As soon as he was outside the door, Frannie scurried over and turned the lock. With a sigh of relief, she sat down on the bed and let the blanket fall from her shoulders. Mr. Scott Winslow would have to break down the door to get to her now. The bed-springs creaked as she moved. She wondered if he was standing outside the door listening. Waiting.

She got up and glanced at her reflection in the bureau mirror. She looked ghastly, her makeup blotchy, her long blond hair disheveled. The flannel shirt hung on her like an oversize nightshirt, and the sweats were baggy. If only she felt free to take a shower and wash her hair. But that was a luxury she couldn't afford right now. Mr. Scott Winslow seemed like a nice enough guy, but one never knew. There was no sense in taking chances and putting herself in harm's way.

The rain was still falling, less forceful than before. It tapped a steady, almost reassuring rhythm on the roof. Weariness enveloped her. She turned off the hurricane lamp and blinked as her eyes got accustomed to the darkness. She climbed onto the bed, curled up on the covers, pulled her blanket over her and fluffed the feather pillow under her head.

For her own safety, she ought to try to stay awake. But the bed felt so comfortable and warm, she could feel her body giving itself up to sleep. "Lord," she whispered, "this isn't how I expected to spend my first night on my own. If Daddy gets wind of it, he's going to tell me to pack up and get myself home. But I can't go back. You know that. Help me, Lord. Sometimes You seem so far away. But I really need You now. I feel so alone. Please keep me safe through the night."

She had intended to say more, but the words died on her lips as she gave herself up to a deep, dreamless slumber.

Frannie's next conscious thought was, Where am I? Sunshine streamed through the windows and seagulls screeched to one another in a blue, cloud-studded sky.

Frannie rolled over and rubbed her eyes. She knew she wasn't at home, but this wasn't her little bungalow either. Then it all came back to her in a rush — the clogged chimney, the smoke, her rescuer bringing her here to his beach house. Everything fell into place. And now it was a glorious morning and she was safe and sound.

A knock sounded on her door, followed by a deep masculine voice. "Miss Rowlands, are you awake?"

She scrambled off the bed and smoothed her rumpled flannel shirt over her sweatpants. "Yes, I'm awake."

"Breakfast will be ready in about ten minutes."

"Breakfast?"

"Do you like coffee?"

"Yes, but —" She unlocked the door, opened it a crack and peered out. Scott Winslow looked even taller and more athletic than she recalled. "I really don't need anything to eat."

"Well, I'm as hungry as a bear. So as long as I'm cooking anyway, you might as well join me for some bacon and eggs."

She caught the aroma of bacon sizzling in a skillet and realized how ravenous she was. "All right. I'll have a little."

"Coffee, too?"

"Decaffeinated?"

"Sorry."

"That's okay. I'll drink whatever you've got."

"I warn you, it's strong stuff. It'll curl your hair."

She grinned. "Then I'll take it. Always did want Shirley Temple ringlets."

He returned her grin. "And you're welcome to use the shower. I'll be busy in the kitchen."

"Thanks. Maybe I will take a quick shower." Her genteel host didn't seem nearly so threatening in the full light of day.

"Soap and shampoo are in the cupboard. Sorry I don't have any of the nice perfumed amenities. Just the basic masculine stuff."

"I'll get by."

It was the fastest shower she'd ever taken. But at least she was clean and her clothes were dry, she mused as she slipped into her own shirt and jeans. Her sneakers were still soggy, and she would have to forgo any makeup, but she sure could use a hairbrush to get out the tangles in her long, thick hair.

She joined Scott in his kitchenette, her hair wrapped in a towel. He was draining the bacon on a paper towel.

"I don't suppose you have an extra hair-brush."

"Top drawer of the bureau. It's even clean. Help yourself."

She returned to the bedroom, opened the drawer and removed the brush, but not before she noticed a snapshot of a young family. Father and mother and two young sons. Was one of those boys Scott Winslow? There was something oddly compelling about the photo. What struck Frannie was that no one in the picture was smiling. The woman stood gazing solemnly at the camera, with one hand on each boy's shoulder. The father stood apart from the others, frowning, gazing off in another direction. Behind them was what appeared to be an immense house, a Spanish-style mansion. If they were fortunate enough to occupy a house like that, why did they look so glum?

Frannie shrugged. It was none of her business. If she had her way, she would probably never encounter her mysterious neighbor again. And yet, she couldn't help feeling curious about him.

As she was about to shut the drawer, Frannie noticed a sketchbook beside the photo. Did that mean Mr. Winslow was an artist like herself? Should I take one little peek inside? she wondered. Why not? It's not like reading private letters, and it might give me a clue to who this man is.

Gently she removed the book, opened the cover and flipped through the pages. The book was filled with sketches of houses, buildings, gardens, playgrounds and trees. They were the work of an untrained hand, and yet they were quite exquisite in their own way. They revealed a man of extraordinary energy and idealism. Not at all the way she perceived Scott Winslow.

His voice sounded from the other room. "Miss Rowlands, did you find the brush? Do you need some help?"

"No, I found it."

She replaced the book, closed the drawer and returned to the living room. She sat down on the couch, unwrapped the towel and shook her hair. Slowly she pulled the brush through the tangled strands. It felt good to be clean again. Even the masculine aroma of the shampoo on her damp hair seemed pleasantly refreshing.

It seemed equally bracing to hear a man at

work in the kitchen. For years now, Frannie had been the one doing kitchen duty at home. This was a pleasant change.

When she had finished brushing her hair, she ambled into the kitchenette and watched as Scott spooned a mound of golden-yellow scrambled eggs into a bowl.

"Looks like you know your way around a kitchen pretty well."

He cast her a boyish glance. "Better wait until you've tried the food before making a judgment call like that."

"If it tastes as good as it looks and smells, you've got it made."

He paused and gave her an approving once-over. "Hey, you clean up pretty good."

She smiled. "That's what my mama always said. Is there anything I can do to help?"

"No, I've got a handle on it."

He carried the eggs and bacon over to a small table by the window. "I've mastered about six dishes, mainly using eggs, potatoes, hamburger and pasta. Anything beyond that and I'm helpless as a baby."

He brought over steaming mugs of coffee and set them down. "As soon as the toast pops up, we're ready to go."

"It smells delicious."

"Then sit down and enjoy it." After fetching the toast, he sat down across from Frannie. "I suppose since you're a minister's daughter, we ought to say grace. Would you like to do the honors?"

She nodded, pleased, and offered a brief prayer. For the next few minutes they concentrated on the food. "It's very good," she told him.

"There's more. Eat up."

"Thanks, but this is plenty. I will have another cup of coffee though. That's potent stuff, but it's delicious."

He got up and filled her mug. "My secret recipe. Actually, I get it at that little market a couple miles from here."

"Oh, yes, I've been there. Nice little place." She debated whether to ask him about his sketches, and decided to chance it. She wouldn't mention the picture though. Somehow she sensed that it was off-limits. "When I got the hairbrush, I noticed your sketchbook. Since I'm an artist, I couldn't resist taking a peek."

He gave her an odd, scrutinizing glance. "So that's what took you so long." She couldn't tell whether he was pleased or upset. "I did those for fun. Just messing around."

"I'm impressed. Have you ever thought about studying art professionally?"

"No. It's just a little hobby of mine. Any talent I have I got from my mother. She was the real thing, an artist of substance. Never got to do much with it, though."

"But you could. I teach an art class at the university. I recognize talent when I see it. You really should consider —"

"I'm not interested, Miss Rowlands."

His tone silenced her. She sipped her coffee, then finished the rest of her eggs.

Scott cleared his throat. "I didn't mean to be so abrupt."

"It's okay. I shouldn't overstep my bounds. Besides, it's time for me to head back to my place and see if I can air out all that smoke."

"I'll help you."

"That's not necessary. You've done quite enough."

He drummed his fingers on the table. "What you said about art classes . . . I'll give it some thought."

She managed a smile. He was trying to make amends. "Good. I'd hate to see talent like yours go to waste."

His face grew ruddy. Frannie saw something she hadn't seen before — vulnerability, hope, delight. "Nobody ever said I had that kind of talent."

"Well, you do. What about your mother?

You said she was an artist. Didn't she praise your drawings?"

"I suppose. But she had her own problems. She was sick a lot. I learned at an early age not to bother her with my concerns."

"Or with your dreams?"

"Yeah, that, too."

"That's a shame. My parents were always there for my sisters and me. We had a very happy life."

"Had?"

"Yes. I'm afraid it's all changed now."

"How so?"

She paused, her spirits darkening. "Daddy's got his new wife and stepdaughter. I really don't feel comfortable with either one of them."

"Is that why you moved into the beach house?"

"That, and the fact that it's time for me to be on my own. I can't be Daddy's little girl forever."

He nodded. "I hear what you're saying."

Frannie sensed that Scott Winslow was speaking out of his own private pain, and it went beyond the death of his mother. "You really do know what I'm saying. You're dealing with more than your mother's death, aren't you?"

His expression changed, as if a veil had

dropped over his features. "We were talking about you, not me, Miss Rowlands."

"I'm sorry. I didn't mean to pry."

"Forget it. I'm a grump in the morning until I've finished my brew." He swallowed the last of his coffee and set the mug down. "There, that's better."

"That's some tonic, Mr. Winslow. If it can change your mood that fast, maybe I'd better get some more for myself."

He sat back in his chair and flexed his shoulders. "Let's drop the formalities. We've spent the night under the same roof . . . and survived. Call me Scott."

"All right. Scott it is. And I'm Frannie." An idea occurred to her. "You know, if you'd like to earn a little extra spending money, I could use a model in my art class."

He grimaced. "Doesn't sound like my kind of thing. Truth is, I like to keep my clothes on in public."

A crimson flush spread over Frannie's face. "Oh, Mr. Win— I mean, Scott — it's not that kind of class."

His face had turned nearly as red as hers. "It's not?"

"No. We don't use nude models. You'd wear a tank top and shorts."

"It's still not my cup of tea. Or coffee, as the case may be."

"It was just a thought."

He chuckled. "If I get that hard up, I'll let you know."

"You do that." She picked up her dishes and carried them over to the sink.

"Don't worry about the dishes. I'll take care of them."

"I don't mind, really. I'm the proverbial mother hen."

"You're the prettiest mother hen I ever saw."

She came back, took his soiled dishes to the sink and turned on the spigot. "You know just what to tell a girl who's wearing yesterday's clothes and not a stitch of makeup."

He got up and grabbed the dish towel. "It's the truth. I wouldn't lie about a thing like that."

"Thanks. Now I don't feel like such a ragamuffin."

When they had finished the dishes, she glanced over at the fireplace, where Ruggs was ensconced in all his furry glory. "Guess I'd better get my dog and go home. I've interrupted your life long enough, Mr. Wins— I mean, Scott."

"No problem. I had no plans for you to interrupt."

A memory stirred at the back of Frannie's

mind. "Your name . . . It somehow rings a bell. Scott Winslow. It seems like I've seen the name in the news."

He stared blankly at her. "I don't think so. I've done nothing noteworthy, except rescue a lady from a smoking chimney, and if that makes tonight's news, I won't know it. No TV."

Frannie rubbed her chin. "Now I remember. Scott Winslow is that billionaire entrepreneur who owns half the real estate in California." She smiled slyly. "You're not that Scott Winslow, are you?"

He chuckled dryly. "If I were, do you think I'd be sitting here?"

She laughed. "Not unless you were totally crazy."

"I'm not that crazy."

She went over and knelt down beside her slumbering pet. "Come on, Ruggs. Wake up, you lazy dog. Time to go home." As she massaged the dog's floppy ears, she looked back at Scott. "Good thing you're not that rich man. I remember the news clip now. Scott Winslow made his fortune providing low-income housing for the poor. But it was so substandard, he created his own slums. A judge sentenced him to live for six months in one of his own buildings that was infested with rats. Can you imagine?"

Scott's countenance darkened. "No, I can't imagine. What kind of monster lives his life like that?"

"I don't know. It's sad, isn't it? How someone like that can totally miss out on the real meaning of life."

Scott flexed his jaw. "Someday he'll get what he deserves."

Ruggs roused himself and stretched, then clambered to his feet and shook his shaggy frame. He yawned and nudged Frannie with his wet nose, as if to say, Okay, I'm ready to go.

Frannie shrugged. "The boss says it's time to leave."

"Guess we can't argue with the boss." Scott walked her and Ruggs to the door and offered his hand as she stepped out onto the porch. "Now you get that chimney cleaned out before you start any more fires, you hear!"

As his hand enveloped hers, she felt a pleasant tickle in her stomach, as if she'd just crested the summit and was on the downward spiral of a roller-coaster ride.

As she stepped off the porch, she shaded her eyes from the blinding sun. "Don't worry, I'll clean my chimney. I promise."

She walked a few yards across the beach, then paused and looked back as Ruggs bounded on ahead. Scott Winslow was still standing on his narrow porch, one hand on the log railing. Something in his stance touched a deep chord in Frannie. She had no words for it, except that the emotions she felt were strong and puzzling. Scott Winslow had aroused her fears, piqued her curiosity and kindled an unexpected tenderness for the reclusive beachcomber.

Chapter Six

Nearly a week passed before Frannie encountered Scott Winslow again. She and Ruggs were walking along the beach at sunset, when she spotted him jogging in a muscle T-shirt and cargo shorts. He waved, and Ruggs went bounding toward him, as if they were long-lost friends.

Scott stooped down and massaged the panting dog. "Hey, Ruggs, ol' boy, how's it going?"

Frannie, in a halter top and stretch shorts, removed her sunglasses and gazed at the strapping jogger. "Look at this! My dog's crazy about you. He never greets me like that."

"You've got to have just the right touch. See, I scratch his ears exactly at the skull. He loves it."

"I knew there had to be a secret to it. I'll have to try it sometime."

"It's easy." Scott straightened and drew close to Frannie, until she could see the sweat beaded on his bronze forehead. He stretched out his hand and gently brushed her hair back with his fingertips, then touched her head just behind her ear. "Right here. This very spot. You just massage in a circular motion. Ruggs will love it."

Frannie drew back with a bemused grin and swung her hair free. "It might be more effective if you demonstrated on the dog."

Scott's dark eyes crinkled merrily. "No, that was just the effect I wanted." He glanced around. "Where you heading?"

"Nowhere special." She followed his gaze. The sun was a huge red ball balanced on an azure-blue skyline. Gulls were circling and screeching to one another, and the waves lapped up over the sand, bathing the soles of her bare feet in cool, refreshing water. "Actually, I'm heading home. Took Ruggs for his usual evening walk. He loves the beach."

Scott raked his fingers through his damp hair. "Did you get your chimney cleaned out?"

"Yes, but we haven't had a cold night since the storm, so I haven't needed it."

"We will again, one of these days." He reached down and gave Ruggs another ear massage. The dog stood rooted to the spot, panting contentedly.

Frannie laughed. "If he were a cat, he'd be purring."

"He is purring. Don't you hear it? That low growl in his throat? He's saying, 'Don't stop. Don't you dare stop!' "

"I don't blame him. You do seem to have the magic touch."

"I told you."

"I haven't seen you since the storm. Are you hiding out?"

His brow furrowed. "Why would you think that? I've been busy. Reading. Thinking. Building a driftwood chair. Jogging at dawn every morning. I haven't seen you out jogging."

"Not at dawn, I can assure you of that."

"Don't knock it until you try it."

"I've been busy getting settled. My dad brought the rest of my stuff last Saturday and helped me set up my studio, so I'm ready to sculpt again."

"Sounds exciting."

"It is to me. Of course, most people think of sculpting with clay as a kindergarten pastime. But I just ignore the rude remarks of the unenlightened masses. Or in this case, I escape to the beach, where I don't have to face them."

"You sound like a girl after my own heart. The life of a loner has its own rewards."

"Then maybe you'll initiate me into the official beachcombers' society."

"I would, if there were one, but we're all fierce individualists. Couldn't get us all together in one room if you tried."

Frannie slipped her sunglasses back on. "Actually, I do have a proposition for you, Scott."

His lips curved in a wily smile. "Go ahead. I haven't heard a good proposition in ages."

"Stop grinning. I'm serious. Remember when I suggested you do some modeling for my class to earn a little extra money?"

"Yes, I remember, and the answer is still no."

"But you haven't heard my offer."

"I have no wish to pose clad or unclad before a bunch of googly-eyed college students."

"I don't want you posing for my class. I want you to pose for . . . me!"

Scott's brows shot up. "You want me to pose just for you? You're kidding!"

"No, I'm not. Last Saturday, when my dad brought me my mail, there was a letter from a Riverside cemetery. They want to commission me to do a Vietnam memorial statue. It would be a wonderful opportunity, and I already have some great ideas. But I'll need someone to pose as a Vietnam soldier."

"What about one of your students?"

"They're all busy with their studies. They wouldn't have time to commit to a project like this."

"But you assume I have the time."

"You could do your thinking and reading while you're posing. I couldn't afford to pay you much, but it would be enough to buy a few groceries and keep your refrigerator stocked. How about it, Scott?"

"You're one persistent gal, aren't you!"

"Tell you what. You'll just have to pose for the initial sketches. Then I can do the actual sculpture from my drawings."

"Where would we work?"

"In the back room at my beach house. Like I said, my dad's got it all set up for me."

Scott scratched his head. "I'll have to think about it."

"Fine. If you're willing, just come by my place tomorrow about ten."

He touched her arm. "But I don't want your money. If I agree to pose, then maybe you can give me some art lessons. Unless you were just being nice when you said you liked my sketches."

Frannie's heart soared. "Oh, I loved your sketches. What a wonderful idea! You'll model and I'll teach. That way we both get what we want. A perfect arrangement!" She held out her hand. "So it's a deal? My place at ten?"

He clasped her hand so firmly, she winced. A light sparkled in his eyes that she hadn't seen before. "Ten sharp it is."

Scott posed for Frannie every day that week, arriving around 10:00 a.m. and leaving by three. He wore a tank top and shorts the first few days, then donned a rented army uniform for the next two. Every day they took a lunch break around noon. She fixed tuna fish sandwiches, opened a can of soup or stuck a frozen pizza in the oven. After lunch, with Ruggs loping at their heels, they walked for a half hour on the beach to clear their heads.

By the end of the week Frannie had completed a dozen drawings, showing Scott from different angles and a variety of poses, some in uniform, some not.

By the middle of the second week, she had done enough sketches to convey the correct musculature in her sculpture, the natural flowing grace of tendons, muscles and sinew. Her excitement for the work blossomed. She couldn't wait to begin building the armature and applying the supple, malleable clay.

But Scott was growing weary of posing. "This is hard work," he told her by the end of the second week. "You get to sit there and draw till your heart's content. I have to stand in awkward poses and hold still for hours on end."

"Just one more day," Frannie begged, "and I'll have all the drawings I need to start work on the sculpture."

"One more day? And what do I get in return?"

"More drawing lessons?"

"You already owe me a dozen lessons."

"Then how about a home-cooked steak dinner? Medium-rare filet mignon, grilled mushrooms and onions, baked potatoes with the works and a fresh garden salad? Guaranteed to be delicious. Don't forget, my family considers me a gourmet cook."

"You really know how to tempt a guy, don't you? Who can resist a tender steak smothered in mushrooms?"

The very next night, Frannie fixed Scott the mouthwatering steak she had promised. He arrived at her cottage just as she was tossing the salad. Dressed in a charcoal-gray shirt and sport coat, he could have passed as a high-level executive of a major corporation.

As he stepped inside, Frannie drew back, giving him the once-over. "Wow, look at you!"

His gaze swept approvingly over her. "You're not so bad yourself."

Frannie made a little curtsy in her sleeveless top and sarong pants. "Looks like we should be doing the town and showing off our fancy duds instead of eating in."

"Next time. My treat."

She returned to her salad. "Don't worry about it. I know money's tight. I can be satisfied with a burger and fries."

"Then you've got a date."

"But not until I've got my armature done. I started today. You can take a look at it. Of course, right now it just looks like a bunch of sticks and chicken wire."

"Don't they call that modern art?"

"You can scoff, but wait till you see the finished product. You'll think you're looking in a mirror. Actually, you'll be cast in bronze, and you will be so fine."

"My secret wish, to be bronzed!"

"Not you, silly. Just the clay model of you."

Scott crouched down and stroked Ruggs

behind the ears. "What do you think of all this nonsense, boy? You think anybody's going to want to see a statue of me in a cemetery?" The shaggy dog barked, pawed the floor and licked Scott's hand. "Okay, so you approve. I guess it's not so bad."

"The money's not so bad, either," said Frannie. "I really wish you'd let me pay you for posing."

"I said no, Frannie."

"I know you like living the simple life, mean and lean and close to the bone, but even you need to eat. If I paid you what you're worth to me, you could have a telephone installed. You wouldn't feel like you're cut off from civilization."

He chuckled. "Who would I call? And who would I want to call me? It's my own choice not to have a phone."

"Or a television, or a computer, or anything else that connects you to the real world." She eyed him curiously. "I wonder sometimes what has made you turn your back on everyone and everything."

"I haven't turned my back on you, Frannie. I rescued you from a smoking chimney, and I've posed for you for two solid, back-breaking weeks."

"And I appreciate your help more than I can say. But I worry about you, Scott. What kind of life do you have, holed up alone in your beach house?"

"I've got the same kind of life you've got. Peace, quiet, solitude. The freedom to come and go as I please." He ambled over to the counter where she was working and helped himself to a wedge of tomato. "So what's the problem, Frannie? We're in the same boat — a boat of our own choosing, I might add."

She sliced an avocado into the salad. "But I haven't narrowed my world to just this cottage. I have a career and a family. I teach an evening class at the university. I go to church on Sunday. I visit my dad. Or at least I will be visiting him next week."

"What's happening next week?"

"A family dinner." Frannie took the salad over to the linen-draped dinette table. "My dad mentioned that the new music director from church will be there. I have a feeling he's pulling one of his matchmaking schemes again."

"Setting you up, huh?"

"My father won't be happy until he has all of his daughters married. Two down, one to go."

"How do you feel about that?"

"To be honest, I have no desire to be tied down to any man."

"So you don't plan to get married?"

"I didn't say that. Maybe someday the right man will come along, but I've got a whole lot of living to do in the meantime." She placed salad bowls and glasses of iced tea on the table. "What about you, Scott? Are you the marrying kind?"

"I thought I was once. But before I got to the altar, I realized it wouldn't work out."

"I'm sorry."

"Don't be. We would have made each other miserable."

Frannie pulled out the two straight-back chairs. "Let's start with the salad while the steak is broiling."

Scott sat down and spread the linen napkin over his lap. "Smells delicious. Suddenly I'm famished."

She looked across the table at him. "Would you like to ask the blessing this time?"

His face reddened slightly. "I'm a little rusty."

"I'm sure the Lord doesn't mind."

"If you say so." He bowed his head and murmured a one-sentence prayer, then said a relieved amen.

Frannie reached across the table and patted his hand. "Thanks. I love to hear a man pray. Reminds me of my dad."

He grimaced. "I haven't had much practice in recent years."

She handed him the salad dressing. "It's never too late to get back in practice. My father's prayers have seen me through more troubles than I could possibly count."

"My mother was like that when I was young. But I think my father wore her down. He scoffed whenever we went to church, told us we were being brainwashed. Said church makes a man weak."

"Your father must have been a very unhappy man."

Scott nodded and turned his attention to his salad, his dark brows shadowing his eyes.

"But your mother took you to church anyway?"

"Yes, when I was a small boy."

"She must have loved you very much."

"She did." He met her gaze and his expression softened. "I loved going."

"Being raised in the church, I never knew anything else."

"You were very fortunate."

"Yes, I guess I was."

"I remember I was about five when I raised my hand in Sunday school and asked Jesus into my heart."

Frannie smiled. "I was five, too. I didn't

understand it all, but I knew something was different in me. I didn't feel lonely anymore. You know, the way you feel alone in the midst of a crowd."

"Yes, I do know."

"It's amazing how you can be so young and yet know that something special has happened to you. I knew Jesus was with me. It was like I was carrying around this special secret in my heart. I wanted to tell everybody. Did you feel that way?"

"I suppose I did. But now, as an adult, I've come to believe that experience was just part of the magic of childhood."

Frannie stared wide-eyed at him. "You can't mean that. Are you saying you've lost your faith?"

"No, not lost it. Just put it in its proper perspective. It was special to me as a child, but not especially relevant to me as a grown man."

"How sad. I admit I haven't felt as close to God these past few years, but the Lord is still very real in my life."

"Good. Don't let anyone talk you out of it."

"You mean . . . like your father talked you out of it?"

"I didn't say that."

"Yes, you did, in so many words."

He nodded toward the broiler. "You'd better check those steaks. Smells like they're done."

For the rest of the meal, they talked about superficial things — the sweltering August heat, the good buys on vegetables at the farmers' market and Frannie's upcoming family dinner.

"So you really think your father is trying to set you up?" asked Scott between bites of baked potato.

"I don't think, I *know.* There's no other reason he would invite an eligible man to dinner. I just wish I could figure out some way to send him a message that I'm not interested."

"What about the direct approach? Just say no."

"Wouldn't work. My father would smile and nod, and then set me up with his version of Mr. Right anyway."

"Then just don't show up at the dinner."

"I can't do that. It would hurt my dad and embarrass his guest. I have no choice but to go and endure the evening."

"Who knows? Maybe you'll like the man."

Frannie speared a tender morsel of steak. "How many ways can I say it? I'm not interested in finding a husband right now. I've got a long way to go to establish myself as a sculptor. What husband will want to wait on dinner while I muck around in the clay?"

A sly smile played on Scott's lips. "If he loves you, he'll have dinner ready for you when you get through mucking around."

Frannie grinned. "Now that sounds like a man I could love!"

"Maybe this fellow your dad picked out is that man."

"No, I don't think so. The thing is, my dad won't even tell the poor guy that he's matching him up with his daughter. It'll all seem like an innocent, ordinary evening. But under the surface my father will be orchestrating everything."

"One of those control freaks, huh?"

"Only when it comes to his darling daughters."

"Can't you just go along with it for one evening?"

"I suppose. I just wish I could show up with a date of my own and cut my dad off at the pass. Then he wouldn't dare try his matchmaking tactics anymore."

Scott chuckled. "Now who's conspiring?"

"Wait, I've got it!" Frannie reached across the table and seized Scott's hand. "You'll be my date!"

He stared blankly at her. "Me?"

"Please! As a favor. Just this once."

"Let me get this straight. You want me to go to your house for dinner and pretend that we're dating?"

"Yes! It'll stop my dad in his tracks. If he thinks I've already met Mr. Right, he won't keep trying to match me up. He'll leave me alone."

"I won't do it."

"Why not?"

"Because I won't lie to your father."

"We won't lie. I'd never lie to him. We'll just act like we like each other and let him draw his own conclusions."

"I do like you, Frannie. I don't have to pretend that."

"And I like you too, Scott. So will you do it?"

"I'll think about it."

Frannie gave him her most beguiling smile. "I made chocolate cheesecake for dessert. Do you suppose that could persuade you?"

Chapter Seven

Andrew Rowlands was on a mission — to bring his wandering daughter back into the fold and get her headed down the matrimonial path. He had even found the perfect mate for his fiercely independent daughter — Wesley Hopkins, the new minister of music at Cornerstone Christian Church. Wesley was a solid, reliable man with a stellar background and an impressive future. Just the sort of man who would take good care of Frannie and balance her mercurial personality with his dependable character.

Of course, if Andrew were honest with himself, he knew he was doing this for himself as much as for Frannie. Since her departure to her beachfront bungalow, Andrew's home wasn't the same. As much as he loved Juliana, he couldn't quite get used to the fact that his house was now occupied by an entirely new group of people. At times, the thought occurred to him, Where have all the others gone — my wife, Mandy, and three daughters? What happened to that life? How is it that I'm still here, but everyone else is different?

It wasn't that he was unhappy with Juliana. He adored her. But since their wedding, she had spent so much time and effort trying to be the perfect minister's wife that she had filled his house with people and activities he didn't recognize — visitors he hardly knew who seemed drawn to Juliana like a magnet, neighborhood women who came for a weekly Bible study and young people who seemed to like congregating at his house after their youth meetings.

It wasn't that Andrew didn't like people. He cared deeply for them. He had been called to serve them as a minister of the Gospel. But he wasn't used to them flocking in and out of his home day and night. At times he quipped that if it got much worse, he would have to install a revolving door.

The simple fact was Andrew was a man who didn't take easily to change. Once the furniture was placed in a certain spot in his house, he wanted it to remain there always. When he had established a daily routine that worked well, he wanted to keep that routine permanently.

But Juliana thrived on rearranging schedules and furniture. Even the sounds and smells in his home were different these days, the voices and conversations louder, the aromas stronger — spicy, garlic-filled pastas, heavy, flowery perfumes.

Juliana was a presence to be reckoned with; with her buoyant personality and natural charisma, she captivated people with a word or a smile. When she entered a room, she took charge of it, dominated it. All eyes turned her way.

Compared to Juliana, his beloved Mandy had been hardly more than a background shadow, small and unassuming, deferent, gentle, quiet, compliant. Of course, Mandy had been a powerhouse of prayer and had accomplished much for her faith, but her deeds were all done behind the scenes, often unnoticed. Andrew hadn't realized Mandy's many achievements until she was gone. The void she had left was enormous.

But now Juliana was the love of his life, and Andrew had to learn a whole new set of responses and expectations. It wasn't that he wanted to tame or change Juliana or make her a carbon copy of Mandy. It was just that he had spent most of his adult life with one kind of woman, and now he had to find a way to accommodate himself to someone exactly the opposite.

Often these days he found himself thinking that life would be easier if Frannie were still at home. All the changes would be balanced with a presence from the past, a familiar face in the kitchen, his own flesh and blood who knew his ways and anticipated his wishes even before he did.

So, even as he invited Frannie to a special family dinner to get acquainted with the new minister of music, he knew his motives weren't unsullied. He wanted his daughter to move back home and begin an approved courtship that he could keep his eye on. He longed to renew that special father-daughter closeness he had come to depend on after Mandy's death. He simply didn't like his youngest trying her wings and soaring into an unknown future without him. The scope of his manipulations made Andrew uncomfortable, but he reminded himself that he had Frannie's best interests at heart. And didn't that justify all his paternal machinations?

The dinner was set for Saturday night, the last week of August. When Frannie mentioned bringing a friend, Andrew had discouraged her, reminding her that the dinner was in honor of the new minister of music. It was a half-truth, the other half being that

Andrew was matchmaking again. But neither Wesley nor Frannie needed to know that minor detail. "Wesley is young and talented and all the way from Michigan," Andrew had told Frannie, "so he doesn't know anyone in California. We want to make him feel welcome, so he'll stay at our church for a long time."

Andrew wasn't sure Frannie was convinced. But tonight he would find out. Now that the big night was here, Andrew felt as nervous as a cat on a hot stove. And it wasn't just because he was afraid Frannie would see through his ploy and resent his meddling.

There was another unknown factor — his reclusive stepdaughter, Belina. As gregarious and outgoing as Juliana was, her daughter was equally withdrawn and aloof. Andrew wasn't even sure she would come to the table. Often she hid out in her room when company came. But perhaps this time Andrew could persuade her to join them. If Frannie saw that Belina missed her and wanted to be friends, perhaps she would give up her beach house and come home.

These thoughts tumbled in Andrew's mind as he showered and dressed for dinner. He knew he should pray about this evening, but he couldn't quite bring himself to say, *Lord, Thy will be done.* His anxieties mounted as he went downstairs and checked on Juliana in the kitchen. She had baked lasagna, her family recipe, and now she was tossing a salad with vinegar and oil.

"It smells delicious in here." Andrew kissed her cheek. "Anything I can do?"

"Take the bottles of sparkling cider out to the table while I put the garlic bread in the oven."

He picked up a bottle in each hand. "Will Belina be joining us for dinner?"

Juliana pursed her ruby-red lips. "I hope so, Andrew. I told her this is a very important dinner for you, that you want her and Frannie to be friends, and you want to make the young music minister feel welcome to our community. So we shall see if she comes down."

The doorbell rang. Andrew glanced at his watch. Someone was ten minutes early. He hoped it was Frannie. But when he opened the door, there stood Wesley Hopkins, tall and lanky as a reed, with a bouquet of yellow roses in his hand and a wide smile on his lips. He looked a bit nervous, but wholesomely attractive in his navy blue blazer, blue shirt and maroon tie. Yes, indeed, he was good son-in-law material — neat, courteous, respectful and dependable.

"I hope I'm not too early, Reverend Rowlands."

"Not at all, Wesley. Come on in. And, please, this is a social evening. Call me Andrew."

"Yes, sir . . . Andrew." With an awkward thrust, he stuck the bouquet under Andrew's nose. "These are for Mrs. Rowlands."

Andrew drew back, rubbed his nose and smiled. "Juliana's in the kitchen working on dinner. But I'm sure she'll love them."

"I hope so. I couldn't decide between pink and yellow. I hope she likes yellow."

"Loves yellow! By the way, my daughter Frannie should be here any moment. I don't think you've met her yet."

"No, sir. I'm looking forward to it. You have a fine family."

"Thank you, Wesley. I'm sure you'll like Frannie. She's a wonderful artist . . . and a superb cook. Almost as good as Juliana. Follow me. We can chat in the living room until dinner's ready."

Andrew stuck the flowers in a glass vase on the buffet, then showed Wesley into the living room. But before they could settle on the sofa, he heard the front door click. He tried to hide his enthusiasm as he said, "Oh, that must be Frannie now."

He strode back to the foyer and arrived

just as Frannie stepped inside. She looked stunning in a simple, belted black sheath and pumps. Wesley couldn't help but fall for her. Andrew was about to give his daughter a welcoming hug when he realized there was someone else just behind her. Andrew gaped at the tall, imposing stranger. He was dressed in a black V-neck shirt and blue blazer and had the tanned face and sun-streaked hair of a surfer.

Andrew gave Frannie a questioning glance.

Embracing him, she whispered, "I said I might bring a friend."

He whispered back, "I assumed you meant someone of the female persuasion."

"Sorry, Daddy. Guess it was a lack of communication." She turned to the robust man beside her. "Scott, this is my father, Reverend Rowlands. Daddy, this is my friend Scott."

Andrew vigorously shook the man's hand, but in his mind's eye he was watching his carefully orchestrated evening collapse around him. "Didn't catch the last name," he murmured politely. But Frannie was already leading her rugged companion into the living room, her arm twined in his. Andrew followed and dutifully introduced Wesley, but his heart wasn't in it now. The evening would be a fiasco, unless he could pawn off this beach bum on someone else . . . like Belina. It was a long shot, but worth the effort.

Slipping his arm around his capricious daughter, Andrew assumed a confidential tone. "Honey, would you mind going upstairs and seeing if you can persuade Belina to come down to dinner? You know how she is around company."

"Sure, Daddy." Frannie turned to her escort. "Be right back, Scott. I want you to meet my stepsister."

By the time Frannie returned downstairs with Belina timidly following behind, Juliana was already putting the salad on the table. Andrew made introductions, giving Belina a fatherly embrace as he did so. She looked quite lovely in a white blouse and pleated jumper, her long black hair framing her delicate, ivory face. These days not even Andrew could tell where her facial scars had been.

But Belina's emotional scars couldn't be erased so easily. She shyly lowered her gaze and kept her hands at her sides as the two men greeted her. Andrew's heart ached for her. If only his stepdaughter could find the courage and confidence to face life head-on. Until she learned to smile and reach out to others, it was unlikely she'd ever find a proper suitor.

The thought made Andrew groan. It struck him suddenly that he had not just one daughter left to marry off, but two! And they both presented him with a monumental challenge.

Juliana's voice broke into his thoughts. "Dinner is served, Andrew. Please bring our guests."

They all gathered around the table and took the chairs Juliana assigned them. Frannie and her young man sat opposite Wesley and Belina. It wasn't the way Andrew had planned, but perhaps Wesley and his daughter would hit it off anyway. Anything was possible.

"Juliana, is there anything I can do to help?" Frannie offered.

"No, dear. Everything is ready. This time you do no work. You just eat and enjoy the meal."

"But what about our spaghetti bibs?" Frannie turned to Scott. "We always wore these huge, homemade bibs on spaghetti night. It was a family tradition."

"Because I am such a klutz," Andrew interjected.

"No bibs anymore," said Juliana with a bright smile. "To me, they are unsuitable for a formal dinner."

After Juliana returned to the kitchen, Frannie mused under her breath, "I always thought they were kind of cute."

Andrew patted his daughter's hand. "Me, too, sweetheart. But let's abide by Juliana's wishes."

Frannie didn't reply, but Andrew could see a shadow of resentment darken her face. Would his darling daughter ever accept Juliana as his wife and the new lady of the house?

"Shall we pray?" he said in his most reverential tone. When he was stymied, he always resorted to his comfortable clergyman's role. Everyone held hands as Andrew said grace. He made a point of asking God's blessing on his two first-time dinner guests, Wesley and Scott.

Minutes later, as his guests consumed their salads, Andrew said conversationally, "So, tell me, Scott, what do you do?"

Scott's eyes remained on his salad as he speared a tomato wedge. "I live in the beach house down the way from Frannie."

"No, I mean, what do you do for a living?"

A long pause. "I'm between jobs right now."

"I see." Andrew's irritation flared. Why

wouldn't the man look him in the eye? "I'm curious. What are you trained to do?"

Finally Scott looked up, his brows shading his dark eyes. "I have a business degree from Stanford."

Andrew whistled through his teeth. "Impressive. A real accomplishment. But I should think, with your background you would have major corporations lining up at your door. And yet you say you're out of work and living in a cottage on the beach?"

"I didn't say 'out of work,' sir. I said, 'between jobs.' "

"Isn't that one and the same?"

Frannie glared at him. "Daddy, please! You're giving Scott the third degree."

Andrew winced inwardly. He knew he was crossing the line, behaving like an overprotective dolt. And yet there was something about this elusive young man that didn't add up. "Sorry, Scott. I didn't mean to be rude. I just like to get to know Frannie's friends. Fathers are like that, you know."

Scott sat back and put down his fork. His expression was inscrutable, but his voice sounded conciliatory. "No problem, Reverend Rowlands. The truth is, my mother died not long ago. We were very close. I needed some time off to regroup and figure out what I want to do with my life."

"I didn't know. I owe you an apology, Scott."

"No apology needed, sir. I trust you can see now why I need some downtime."

"I certainly can, Scott." Andrew sipped his sparkling cider, then asked with a casual air, "So what do you hope to do when you get back into the swim of things?"

Frannie interrupted. "Scott's quite an artist, Daddy. You should see the buildings and houses he draws. And the lovely gardens and trees."

"An artist, are you? That's quite a leap from a business degree."

"Art is my hobby, Reverend Rowlands. Only a hobby. And I'm really not very good at it, no matter what Frannie says."

"That's not true, Scott. You have a lot of natural ability. And by the time we've finished our lessons, you'll be drawing like a professional."

Andrew's eyes narrowed. "You're giving him art lessons?"

"Yes, Daddy. And he's posing for me."

"Posing for you?"

"Oh, Daddy, it's just for the commission I'm doing for the Riverside cemetery. I needed someone to pose as a Vietnam soldier. Scott is an excellent model."

Before Andrew could utter another word, Frannie looked across the table at Wesley Hopkins. "So, Wesley, how do you like California?"

A wide grin spread across the man's narrow face. "I have mixed feelings, Miss Rowlands."

"Frannie, please."

"I love the weather and the scenery, Frannie. The ocean and palm trees and mountains. But I haven't got the hang of the freeway system yet. I hold my breath every time I head for an on-ramp. And the traffic! I don't know how veteran commuters stand it."

"It can drive you to distraction," Frannie agreed. "That's another reason I love living at my beach house. I can pretend I'm the only person in the world."

Wesley beamed. "You make it sound quite appealing, Frannie."

Andrew knew the young music director was hooked when he added, "Maybe I'll drop in on you sometime and see what it's like firsthand. I'd phone first, of course."

Andrew could see that Wesley's offer didn't sit well with his daughter.

Frannie cast a quizzical glance at Scott, then looked over at Belina, who was staring down at her plate and seemed unaware of the entire conversation. In an excessively bright voice, Frannie said, "Belina, didn't you say you wanted to come see my new beach house?"

Belina looked up in bewilderment, as if rousing herself from a daydream. "Did I say that?"

"I'm sure you did." As Frannie rushed on, Andrew could almost see the gears turning in her mind. "Why don't you come and bring Wesley sometime, Belina? Maybe Scott could come over too, and the four of us could have lunch or dinner together."

Belina's hand flew to her mouth. "No, I couldn't, really."

"Oh, but it would be fun!" said Wesley, his face lighting up. "Please, Belina. I would be honored if you'd accompany me to your sister's place. I'm even willing to tackle these crazy freeways, if you'll be my navigator."

Belina's face reddened. She seemed to be shrinking in her chair. Andrew had the surreal sensation that if she continued recoiling into herself, she would simply disappear. He wanted to rescue his mortified stepdaughter, but, for once in his life, his mind was a blank.

Juliana spoke up and saved the day, her voice ebullient as a song. "That is a wonderful idea, Frannie. Of course you will go, Belina. You will have a splendid time. You and Wesley are very much alike."

"Oh, Mama, please! You're embarrassing me!"

"But it's true, child. You both love music. You both have fine voices. You will be good for each other!"

"Then it's settled." Relief colored Frannie's voice. With a glance at Andrew that blended triumph and defiance, she placed her hand over Scott's, as if the two were certainly more than friends. "The four of us will have great fun together, Daddy."

Andrew couldn't help noticing the way Scott slipped his arm possessively around Frannie's shoulder, as if they were already a couple planning a future together. A sour taste rose in his throat. Juliana hadn't even served the lasagna yet, and already he had indigestion.

And no wonder! For all of his matchmaking efforts, it appeared that his precious daughter was going to end up at the altar with a shiftless beachcomber!

Chapter Eight

When Frannie awoke the next morning, a smidgen of guilt pinched her thoughts. She couldn't get back to sleep. Last night she had deliberately misled her father about Scott, and now he was probably afraid she would marry a drifter. If she wanted a clear conscience, she would have to phone and reassure him that she and Scott were only friends. But maybe she'd give her dad another hour or so to stew about it first.

Since she couldn't sleep anyway, Frannie got up, put on a halter top, shorts and sneakers and roused Ruggs from his bed by the fireplace. "Come on, boy. Let's go take a run on the beach. We'll both feel better with some sun and fresh air."

The sun was already shimmering on the waves as she and Ruggs tromped over the packed sand to the water's edge. She kicked off her sneakers and waded into the water.

"Try it, Ruggsy. The water's warm."

With a low growl, Ruggs backed up and pawed at the ground.

She ruffled his furry head. "Don't worry, I'm not going to drag you in. Come on, we'll jog in the sand."

She broke into a run along the beach and Ruggs bounded after her, yipping happily. The salty breeze caressed her face and fanned her hair as she quickened her pace. No ambling gait today; she was ready for a brisk sprint.

Suddenly she was aware of someone running with her, just a step behind. She slowed and glanced back, then stopped in her tracks. "Scott, you startled me."

He grinned and raked back his hair from his tanned face. He was wearing sweats and a tank top that showed off his glistening muscles. "Didn't mean to scare you. Just surprised to see you on the beach this early."

She looked up at him, shading her eyes from the sun. "Couldn't sleep. So thought I'd take Ruggs for a run. He's getting to be such a lazy pooch."

"Mind if I join you?"

"Be my guest."

"I'll race you to that palm tree by the rocky ledge."

"That's a good half mile."

"Too much for you, huh?"

"I didn't say that."

"Then let's try it."

They bolted forward at the same time and ran side by side, with Ruggs bringing up the rear. All too quickly Scott raced ahead and kept the lead by several yards. He was waiting for her at the palm tree, smiling triumphantly. By the time she reached the tree, Frannie's rib cage ached. She bent over, her hands on her knees, panting, catching her breath. Then she collapsed on the sand and lay on her back, her heart pounding like a jackhammer.

Ruggs assumed this was a game and plopped his shaggy hide down on top of her.

"No, Ruggsy, get off!"

Scott came to her rescue. "Move it, boy. The lady said no!"

As Ruggs skulked off to examine a soggy rope of seaweed, Scott stretched out on the damp sand beside Frannie. He cupped his hands behind his head and gazed up at the sun-washed sky. "Guess I gave you a run for your money."

She turned her face to his. "Didn't know there was any money involved."

"But if there had been —"

"What? You would have let me win the race?"

"No chance. I have a very competitive spirit."

"So I see."

He grinned. "Don't tell me you're upset with me."

"Of course not. Why would I be upset?" She gave him a sly grin. "But if you were a gentleman, you would have let me win."

"No way!" He tossed a handful of sand on her bare legs. "You're just a poor sport!"

"I am not!" She grabbed a fistful of sand and threw it at his chest.

He rolled over on one elbow and shot her a challenging glance. "So you wanna fight?"

"Sure!" She scooped up more sand. Before she could toss it, he lunged forward and grabbed her wrists. "Oh, no, you don't!"

She struggled to free herself, but he held her fast. She kicked at his shin, but he rolled over and pulled her with him until she found herself in his arms, their faces only inches apart, his breath warm on her cheek.

Promptly she wriggled free and he released her. He hoisted himself up and brushed off the sand. He looked as taken off guard as she was. "I'm sorry, Frannie. I didn't mean to —"

She scrambled to her feet, her pulse

quickening. "It's okay, Scott. I'm fine. No harm done."

"Good. I hope you didn't think I was —"

"No, I didn't. Didn't think a thing."

"Because I wasn't trying —"

"Of course you weren't." She turned to Ruggs, who had his nose buried in slimy green seaweed. "Come on, boy. Time to head home. I've got work to do."

Scott fell into step beside her. "I'll walk you back."

"You don't have to."

"I'm going in the same direction."

"Okay. But let's take it at a slower pace this time."

He nodded. "Much slower."

She glanced over at him. "I hate to say this, but I'm feeling a little guilty this morning."

"Guilty? Why?"

"For giving my dad the wrong impression about us."

"You said you wanted to discourage his matchmaking schemes. And I think we were quite convincing, don't you? He's expecting wedding bells any day now. He's not a happy camper."

"I know. But I handled it the wrong way. I shouldn't have misled him. He's a wonderful father, and I adore him."

"Then tell him the truth. We're friends. Period."

"I will. I'm going to phone him today. But he's got to understand that I'm a grown woman who wants to make her own choices. He can't keep interfering in my life and thinking he knows what's best for me."

"What about this double date you've set up with your stepsister and that Wesley fellow?"

"Oops, I forgot. I should keep my word. Would you mind?"

He winked at her. "What are friends for?"

"I'll talk to Belina when I phone my dad. She may back out of the date anyway. She's so painfully shy. You'd think she was still disabled and disfigured."

"Maybe she is. On the inside. Emotional wounds take a lot longer to heal than physical ones."

Frannie flashed Scott an approving smile. "You're pretty wise for a man who claims to be a simple beachcomber."

"Solitude is good for the soul."

"Yes, I'm learning that, too."

They had arrived at Frannie's bungalow, and Ruggs was pawing at the door.

Frannie opened it, then glanced back at Scott. "What about Friday night? We could barbecue steaks outside on the grill."

"Sounds good to me. Run it by your stepsister and let me know."

To Frannie's surprise, Belina agreed to the double date. "Do you want to phone Wesley," Frannie asked her, "or should I call him?"

"Would you mind phoning him? I don't think I could work up the courage."

Frannie smiled at the undercurrent of excitement in Belina's soft, breathy voice. "Don't worry, I'll arrange everything. I'll tell Wesley to pick you up around six. Is that okay?"

"Yes, Frannie. Thank you. You don't know what this means to me."

"No problem, Belina. I'm looking forward to it."

As Frannie clicked off her cell phone, she felt a peculiar sense of satisfaction. This date obviously meant more to Belina than Frannie could have imagined. Maybe Belina wasn't the sour-faced stick-in-the-mud that Frannie had assumed. Maybe it wasn't her choice to be a recluse. She had lived a solitary existence for so long, maybe it was all she knew.

The thought passed through Frannie's mind, Maybe it's not too late to be a sister to this reclusive girl. But did she even want to be close to Belina? She had moved out of her father's house partly to get away from her remote stepsister. But what if Belina wasn't really odd at all? What if she was just sad and lonely and afraid?

All day long on Friday, Frannie kept expecting Belina to phone and say she had canceled her dinner date with Wesley. But no call came. Looks like the dinner is on, Frannie mused as she put large russet potatoes in the oven to bake, then changed into a mint-green halter dress.

At six-thirty, Scott arrived, looking startlingly handsome in a blue sport shirt and navy khaki slacks. He handed Frannie a bouquet of yellow daisies and salmon-pink baby roses in a clear, cut-glass vase. "Fresh flowers for the hostess," he murmured as he stepped inside.

Ruggs bounded toward him and eagerly licked his hand. Scott's fingers moved instinctively to the back of Ruggs's ears.

"Am I early? Or has the other couple bowed out after all?"

"No, I'm expecting them any moment now." Frannie took the vase of flowers and set it in the center of her linen-draped table. "Thank you, Scott. Now the table is perfect! That was so thoughtful of you."

He grinned and nudged her chin playfully. "I figured we might as well do this evening up right. This might be our only official date, since, as we agreed, we're just friends."

She stifled a chuckle. "That doesn't mean we can't see each other. Friends spend time together."

"Good. I'm glad we clarified that, because solitude has lost its luster since you came along."

She met his gaze with a sly grin. "Are you saying you enjoy my company?"

His dark eyes crinkled. "And that's quite an admission coming from a confirmed hermit like myself."

"Really? Well, I —"

Ruggs severed their conversation with a sudden frenzy of barking. He dashed back and forth from Frannie to the door, his thick fur flying.

"Looks like we've got company." Scott followed Frannie to the door. Her two guests stood on the small porch — Wesley, in a pullover brown shirt and slacks, towering over Belina in a simple blue A-line dress and sandals. With her long ebony hair curled around her delicate face, Belina had never looked prettier.

Frannie smiled. "Welcome to my humble abode!"

As they stepped inside, Belina uttered a

little exclamation of pleasure. “This is so quaint. And the ocean is just outside your door. I see why you love living here.”

Wesley handed Frannie a box of foil-wrapped chocolates. “Hope you have a sweet tooth.”

“I do, but I don’t mind sharing these with everyone.”

“You’ve got a charming, comfortable little place here.”

“Thank you, Wesley. I like it. Please, sit down. Dinner’s almost ready.”

“May I help?” Belina asked, her voice almost a whisper.

Frannie nodded toward the kitchenette. “There’s not much room for two cooks. But you could toss the salad while I sauté the mushrooms.”

Scott placed a hand on Frannie’s shoulder. “And I’ll get the fire started in the grill. You bring out the steaks.”

To Frannie’s relief, the meal went without a hitch, and everyone seemed to enjoy it. While she served a fresh strawberry pie for dessert, Belina cleared the table.

When they were out of earshot of the men, Belina said under her breath, “Frannie, I’ve never had so much fun. Thank you for inviting us.”

“I’m glad you could come.”

"I can see why you love Scott. He's such a kind, charming man. And I can tell he's very fond of you, too."

Frannie's breath caught momentarily. She nearly dropped the steaming coffeepot she held in her hand. How could Belina think she loved Scott or that he cared about her? "Didn't my dad tell you? Scott and I were just pretending to be a couple to get my dad off his matchmaking high horse."

Belina's dark eyes met Frannie's, then her lashes lowered diffidently. "I don't mean to speak out of turn. But perhaps you two are fooling yourselves, not your father. When I look at you, I see a couple."

"I'm sorry, Belina. You're mistaken." Frannie hurried back to the table with the coffeepot, but Belina's words lingered in her mind: *I can see why you love Scott. . . . And I can tell he's very fond of you, too.*

"Who wants coffee?" Frannie asked, too brightly.

Scott held out his cup. "I'll have some."

Frannie's hand shook slightly as she poured, and the hot liquid sloshed outside the cup. "I'm sorry, Scott. I'm suddenly all thumbs."

"No problem. Want me to pour?"

She gave him the coffeepot and sat down,

hoping he wouldn't think her nervousness had anything to do with him.

Wesley gave Frannie an approving nod. "This strawberry pie is out of this world. You should go into business."

"Then I'd never have time to sculpt."

Wesley forked up another ripe, red berry. "If you show the world what you can do with a mound of berries, men will beat a path to your door."

Frannie laughed. "My reason for moving here was to find some peace and solitude. Men beating a path to my door definitely doesn't fit that image. Besides, I'd much rather sink my hands in a mound of clay than a mound of strawberries."

"But the clay isn't nearly so delicious," said Scott, tossing her a sly smile. "Believe me, I know."

"Scott is posing for me," Frannie explained. "Before you go, I'll show you the sculpture. It's nearly completed."

"I would love to see it." Belina's voice was hushed, soft as the air.

Wesley turned to Belina and said, "But first, it's your turn. You haven't told us much about yourself, Miss Pagliarulo."

"It's Belina, please."

"Very well, Belina. What's your favorite pastime?"

Her face reddened. "I don't know. I love to read. I love to dream. And I love music."

"Do you sing?" Wesley leaned close to Belina with a conspiratorial air. "You must sing. You're a member of the Pagliarulo family. Your mother and brother have exceptional voices. Surely you sing, too."

Belina lifted her fingers to her lips, as if to muffle her reply. "I sing a little. But only for myself."

"That's hardly fair," said Wesley, "to deprive the world of your singing voice. Would you consider joining the church choir?"

Belina lowered her head and rocked back in her chair. "I couldn't. I'm sorry."

"No, I'm the one who's sorry," said Wesley. "You would add so much to our choir." He glanced over at Frannie. "Some of our choir members have more enthusiasm than talent."

"Yes, I've heard them." Frannie reached over and patted her stepsister's hand. "Couldn't you just think about it, Belina? Give it a try. You might enjoy it."

"I — I'll think about it, but I can't promise —"

"Wonderful!" Wesley clasped Belina's arm with an exuberance that startled her. "I welcome you to the choir of Cornerstone Christian Church!"

Scott raised his coffee cup in a congratulatory salute.

Belina shook her head. "I didn't say yes."

Wesley reminded her, "But you didn't say no."

When they had finished their dessert and coffee, Frannie suggested, "Why don't we take a walk on the beach? The house is a little warm, and there's a full moon out tonight."

"A wonderful idea." Wesley pushed back his chair, stood and pulled out Belina's chair. "A moonlight stroll is the perfect way to end the evening."

Frannie and Scott exchanged amused glances, as if to say, Look at this! A romance is brewing! Scott got up and helped Frannie out of her chair, and the foursome headed outside, with Ruggs trotting close behind them.

They walked down to the beach and stood close enough to the water to feel the salt spray from the whitecaps rolling in. Belina slipped off her sandals and waded into the water, holding her skirt up.

"Be careful." Wesley followed her to the water's edge. "Don't fall in."

"Don't worry. I love the water! It's still warm from the heat of the day. Come join me!"

With a titter of laughter, Frannie kicked off her sandals and waded into the sea. "Come on in, you guys. It's great!"

Scott and Wesley exchanged dubious glances, then shrugged, removed their shoes and rolled up their pant legs.

"No splashing," Scott warned Frannie as he slogged out to meet her. "I don't want a replay of the night we met."

"What night was that?" asked Belina.

"The wettest night of the year." Frannie gave a quick recap of how Scott had saved her from her smoky cottage and the two had gotten drenched in the downpour. "He was a regular Sir Galahad. I don't know what I would have done without him."

Scott clasped her hand and swung it loosely between them. "But she had to promise not to set any more fires."

"And I haven't touched so much as a match since then." Frannie bent down and ran her fingers through the foamy waves that crescendoed against her bare legs. "Isn't this the best? Having the whole Pacific Ocean for a front yard?"

"I love it!" Belina raised her arms to the sky, her long raven hair rippling in the breeze. "Look, the moon is so bright, the ocean looks like it's glittering with diamonds."

Frannie lifted her skirt and waded in deeper, one hand still holding Scott's for support. "We should change into our swimsuits and have a midnight dip."

"No way." Scott's fingers tightened around her hand. "This is as far as I go."

She playfully yanked his hand. "Come on. I dare you. Just a little farther." She took another step and the sand gave way to a slippery patch of seaweed. As the slimy tentacles wrapped around her ankles, she swayed and nearly lost her footing.

Suddenly two strong arms seized her around the waist and held her fast. Flustered, she gazed up into Scott's dark, snapping eyes. "Didn't I warn you? You almost went under."

She clung to him as she kicked away the stringy seaweed. He kept his arm around her as he led her back to shore. Belina and Wesley followed. They gathered their shoes, socks and sandals, and when they reached dry sand, they sat down.

Wesley unrolled his pant legs and wiggled his bare toes. "Got to dry these tootsies off before I put on my socks."

"It's nice here," said Belina. "I don't want to go back inside." She looked at Wesley, beside her. "When I couldn't walk, my brother would carry me in his arms on the beach. Sometimes we'd go out in the middle of the night, when no one was around. Those times on the beach are my best memories."

Wesley moved closer. "I'd like to hear more about your life, Belina."

Frannie nodded. "You've never talked much about the past."

Belina drew a circle in the sand and turned it into a sad face. "Most of it was too painful. It's not easy to find the words. It was a very lonely existence."

"But not anymore, Belina. We won't let you be lonely." Wesley leaned over, erased the lines in the sand and made a smiling face. "God willing, from now on, there will be only happy faces for you."

Belinda looked around at each of them, tears glistening in her eyes. "I have never had friends. Until now."

"You not only have friends," said Frannie over a sudden lump in her throat. "Don't forget, you have a sister, too."

Belina's countenance shone, as if illuminated with moon glow. "Thank you, Frannie. I didn't think you wanted another sister."

Frannie blinked self-consciously. "I didn't know it, either, until now."

"This is turning into an evening of quiet revelations," noted Wesley. "Say, I have an idea. Why don't we play one of those silly ice-breaker games they play at parties?"

"What?" Frannie challenged. "You mean, truth or dare?"

"No, not exactly." Wesley sat forward and wrapped his arms around his long, narrow legs. "We'll all answer the same question, something philosophical, like 'What is your secret desire?' "

"Count me out," said Scott. "I'm not good at party games."

Wesley made a soft chuckling sound low in his throat. "Come on, it won't be so bad. How about this? What achievement would you most like to accomplish in your lifetime if money and circumstances weren't an issue?"

"And talent weren't an issue, either?" Scott smirked.

"Whatever. Okay, it's my idea, so I'll start. I'd like to compose a work of music, an oratorio, that would turn people's hearts to God the way *The Messiah* has."

Belina touched his arm. "What a wonderful goal, Wesley."

"Thank you." He clasped her hand, intertwining his fingers with hers. "Okay, who's next?"

Frannie lifted her hand. "Okay, I've got it. I would like to create a work of art that points people to God, like Michelangelo's Sistine ceiling."

Scott squeezed her shoulder. "And you may do that someday with your sculpture."

"I hope so. What about you, Scott?"

"No, let's just skip me, okay? It's not worth mentioning."

"Of course it is," said Wesley. "Come on, Scott, we'd all like to hear."

Scott looked thoughtful for a minute. When he finally spoke, his voice was husky. "I'd like to create housing developments where even poor people would be surrounded by beauty. Mothers would have their own gardens, children their own playgrounds, teenagers a place to play ball. And there would be a park where lovers could stroll, people could jog and old men could sit on benches and watch the world go by." He paused and looked away, as if embarrassed by his own impassioned words.

Frannie reached over and turned his face toward hers. "That's a beautiful thought, Scott. Who knows? Maybe someday you'll make that dream come true."

He grinned sheepishly. "Not at the rate I'm going."

"We all have to live by our dreams," said Frannie softly. "When we stop dreaming, we're dead."

"What about you, Belina?" said Wesley. "We haven't heard your wish."

She lowered her gaze. "It's nothing so grand as yours."

Wesley urged her on. "Let us be the judge of that."

"All right, I will tell you. But don't laugh."

"We would never laugh," Frannie assured her.

"It's just a little thing." Belina's voice was as soft and light as the breeze. "I would like to find the courage to stand before a congregation and sing without terror in my heart."

"Beautiful, Belina. Such a pure, sweet wish." Wesley moved beside her, until their arms were touching. "If you let me, I will help you make that wish come true."

As Wesley and Belina exchanged lingering smiles, Frannie had a sudden insight into what inspired her father's matchmaking efforts. Making someone happy — or even better, *two* someones — gave a person a real adrenaline rush.

Or was this rush of emotion coming from somewhere else? Frannie looked up at Scott. He was smiling down at her. Something in his eyes transfixed her. It was as if he were reading her very thoughts, listening to her pounding heart. The silent beat was saying, Frannie, this is a man you could love!

Chapter Nine

To keep her mind off Scott, Frannie threw herself into her work. She completed her bust of Longfellow and delivered it to the La Jolla's Children's Museum the first week of September. Her sculpture of the Vietnam soldier was due at the kiln by the middle of September, where it would be fired and then cast in bronze for the final memorial statue. But Frannie couldn't get the finishing touches just the way she wanted them. There was something missing in the soldier's face — a rugged intensity, a raw courage that she had been trying for days to capture. Her sketches weren't enough to go by now. She needed a flesh-and-blood person for the subtle nuances of shape, form and expression. She needed Scott.

Early on a Tuesday afternoon she tramped over to his cottage, wishing as she trudged under the blazing sun that the man would at least invest in a cell phone. It was ridiculous that there was no way to contact him, except to show up at his door.

As she scaled his sagging porch steps, it occurred to her that he probably wasn't home anyway. In midday he would probably be out collecting driftwood for his innovative, one-of-a-kind furniture. Or selling firewood to passersby on the street. It was odd that a man of Scott's refinement and intellect was satisfied living the life of a beach bum.

But who was Frannie to judge? Hadn't she chosen the same sort of life for herself? Still, it bothered her that Scott didn't aspire to a higher calling or a professional career. If she were honest with herself, she had to admit that Scott's lack of ambition vexed her not just for his sake, but for her own.

Ever since the night of their double date with Wesley and Belina, Frannie hadn't been able to get Scott out of her mind. What concerned her most was that she found herself thinking of him, not just as a neighbor and friend, but as a man she could fall in love with.

Naturally Frannie had experienced her share of high school and college crushes. But until now she had never found a man she seriously considered spending her life with. It amazed her that she was entertaining such thoughts about Scott, a man seemingly without a past, without a career, without a future. In the few weeks she had known him, she knew almost nothing about him.

Maybe she was just going through a phase, or subconsciously retaliating against her father for his matchmaking schemes. Maybe she was drawn to Scott simply because he was so mysterious and charming. Whatever was prompting this silly infatuation, she knew one thing for sure: Scott Winslow was definitely not husband material.

As she knocked soundly on his door, she chided herself for harboring such foolish sentiments. If Scott guessed what she was feeling, he would probably burst into laughter or take off running in the opposite direction. There was no way on earth she would ever confide her schoolgirl fantasies to him.

The door opened suddenly, catching Frannie unawares. She stepped back, startled, her hand flying to her throat. Scott stared back at her, a puzzled expression on his face.

"Frannie, you okay?"

She caught the wood railing and inhaled

sharply. "I — I'm fine. I didn't expect to see you there."

"Then why are you here knocking on my door?"

"I mean, I needed to see you. But I didn't think you'd be home."

He shrugged and stepped aside. "You're not making any sense, but come on in."

She entered the small bungalow and gazed around, as if looking for clues. There had to be something in this house that told her who this man was. Someday she'd find it. "I hope I'm not disturbing you." She noticed his open Bible on the table. "Were you reading?"

"As a matter of fact, I was. Sit down at the table and join me."

She pulled out the chair and sat down. "You seem to spend a lot of time reading the Bible."

"I've read it through twice since I moved here seven months ago."

"Really? I'm impressed. It takes me a year to read through it once."

He thrummed his fingers on the tissue-thin pages. "I came to this cabin to search for truth. And this book is the only place I know to find it."

She nodded. "My father would be pleased to hear you say that."

"Your father?" He eyed her curiously. "What about you, Frannie?"

"I'm pleased, too."

"Being a minister's daughter, you must know the Scriptures very well."

She shifted uneasily. "Not as well as I should. Being a minister's daughter doesn't give me an inside track with God."

"I know that. Scripture says that whoever will may come. Even a beachcomber who hasn't been to church since he was young. But you have a head start on most of us, Frannie. You've been brought up in the church."

"Sometimes you take for granted what you've always had."

"Is that what you've done with your faith?"

"I suppose so. I figured Daddy would get it right for the rest of us. It's not that I don't believe all the right things. But, to be honest, God has never seemed especially close."

Scott flipped through several pages. "I've been reading the letters of the apostle Paul. He talks about knowing Christ personally and having daily fellowship with Him. He says when we become a believer, Christ's Spirit comes and resides within us and communes directly with us."

"Yes, that's true."

"I experienced that when I was a child and invited Jesus to be my Savior. For a long time after that I felt His presence. But somewhere along the line, I lost that sense of Him in my life."

"He's still there, Scott. Maybe you just stopped listening."

"Yes, I'm sure that's it. Because I've started listening again, Frannie, and I know He's still there." He tapped his chest. "He's still in here. And, incredibly, I've begun to feel His love again. But I've got a lot of catching up to do."

"I'm happy for you, Scott. Having faith is a wonderful gift. Sometimes I wish I could be more like my father and experience that kind of vibrant, personal walk with God."

Scott's dark eyes drilled into hers. "Why can't you?"

She shrugged, suddenly uncomfortable. "I suppose I could. I guess I just haven't made God my priority."

Scott pushed the Bible toward her. "Let's work on it together, okay?"

She gave him a baffled look. "What are you talking about?"

He flashed her a bemused grin. "I'm suggesting we get together and study the Bible now and then. You could share your vast wisdom with me, and I could be, um, immensely grateful. And who knows? Maybe we could even try praying together. Like they do in church."

"Scott, why don't you just come with me to church?"

His brows furrowed. "No, Frannie. I can't. I'm not ready for that."

"Not ready for what? Mingling with the rest of humanity? Exposing yourself to the civilized world?" Her frustration spilled out in a rush of words. "What's wrong with you, Scott? Why do you avoid people? Who are you hiding from?"

Scott pushed back his chair, sprang to his feet and strode over to the window. "You don't understand, Frannie."

"Then explain it so I can understand. We're friends, Scott, and yet I feel like you're a stranger."

He gazed out the window, then back at her. "Someday I'll tell you everything. But until then, you have to trust me. That's all I can say right now."

"You haven't said anything. How do I know you're not a — an ax murderer or something?"

He came back over to the table, sat down and clasped her hands in his. "Do I look like an ax murderer?"

"I don't know. I've never met one."

"Well, take my word for it, I'm not. You say I'm a stranger. But you know all the important things about me. I mind my own business and don't bother anyone. I take pity on strangers who knock on my door in the middle of the night. I love God and the world He's created. I love your friends. I love your dog. I love you."

She gaped at him, speechless.

A wily smile played on his lips. "I didn't mean to let that slip out. Forget I said it, okay?"

She looked away, heat rising in her cheeks. In a high, thin voice she said, "I'd be glad to get together and study the Bible with you, Scott."

"Great! We can start now if you like."

"I would, except . . . I came to ask a favor."

"Well, one good turn deserves another."

"I need you to pose for me again. Just for a day or two. I'm completing my commission for the Riverside cemetery, and I have some finishing touches. I can't get the face quite right. My Vietnam soldier just doesn't look soldierly enough. Would you mind coming over?"

Scott gave her a sly wink. "Another thing you know about me, Frannie. When a lady's in distress, I always come running."

True to his word, the next day, Scott showed up at Frannie's beach house at 10:00 a.m. sharp to pose for the sculpture. Frannie's delight knew no bounds. Being able to study — and actually touch — the solid planes and angles of Scott's sturdy face gave her exactly what she needed, what she had been struggling to achieve. As her trained fingers massaged the supple clay, she began to capture the pathos, strength and rugged humanity of her soldier.

Two days later, when she gazed at the final result, she felt the keen inrush of satisfaction, gratitude and pride. She had been true to her original vision. She had poured herself into this work of clay, had given it everything she had. It was part of her, an expression of her very soul, that part of herself that she couldn't express in any other way.

But what struck her most of all was that her clay soldier represented her blossoming feelings for Scott Winslow. The affection she had for the work, she also had for the man. By creating his image in clay, she had glimpsed the inner person, as well. And she liked what she saw.

"So what do you think of it?" she asked Scott as she washed the clay from her hands.

He walked around the nearly life-size sculpture, studying it from different angles as he rubbed his broad chin. "So that's how you see me? I'm impressed. And flattered. You have me looking downright heroic, noble, larger than life."

She gave him a teasing smile. "Are you saying you aren't all those things?"

He grimaced. "Not by a long shot."

She removed her smock and tossed it on her worktable. "Come with me. You deserve some sustenance after all your hours of posing."

He followed her down the hall to her kitchenette. "What about you? You did all the work. Let me take you to dinner."

She looked at him in surprise. "You're going to give up your solitary existence long enough to eat dinner in a public restaurant?"

"You make me sound like an eccentric old hermit."

She laughed. "Aren't you? Not old, of course. But a hermit, for sure." She paused. "But you haven't always been, have you?"

"Neither have you."

"Touché."

"So do we go to dinner or not?"

She peeked inside her cupboard. "I guess so. Unless you'd like some boxed macaroni."

"I pass."

"Okay, dinner out, then. But I'll have to get cleaned up. I've got clay in my hair and up to my elbows."

He stepped forward and swiped his index finger across her cheekbone. "And you've got a streak or two of mud — I mean, clay — on your face, young lady."

"So give me an hour to shower and change clothes."

"That'll give me time to change, too."

She walked him to the door. "Where are we going?"

"I have a place in mind. It'll be a surprise, okay?"

She smiled, noticing the way his eyes twinkled when he said the word *surprise.* "I'm looking forward to it, Scott."

"I'll pick you up in an hour."

She had just put the finishing touches on her makeup and run a brush through her long blond hair, when she heard Scott's familiar knock. Ruggs bounded to the door and barked while she stole a glance in the mirror at her tailored crepe blazer and trousers. The dusty rose outfit was elegant and yet feminine, exactly right for their first official date.

She tried to ignore her quickening pulse as she greeted him. Why was she feeling nervous when she had just seen him an hour ago? Maybe because he looked stunning in his casual brown shirt and tan sport coat. He ambled inside, stroked Ruggs behind the ears and bent over and brushed a kiss on her cheek. Another first!

She felt the color rise in her face. "You look great. Must be we're passing up the fast-food joints tonight."

He touched her hair with the tips of his fingers. "The way you look, there's not a restaurant in town ritzy enough."

She laughed lightly. "I bet you say that to all your dates."

"You're my first date in over six months."

"I'm flattered."

He walked her out to his vehicle, a vintage black sports car, and opened the door for her. As he pulled out into the street, she ran her hand over the leather upholstery. "With a classic car like this, you must have won some sweepstakes."

"Not really. This is my one and only indulgence."

"I've seen you driving by. I wondered if I'd ever get to ride in it."

"You should have asked."

"I wasn't sure it was yours."

"You think I stole it?"

"Of course not. But it's not the sort of car

you can afford on a beachcomber's salary."

"I don't know. I've made some pretty good money on some of my driftwood furniture."

"Maybe I'd better give up sculpting and start collecting driftwood with you."

"Anytime."

She gazed out the window. "Where are we going?"

"To Diego's, a little Mexican restaurant in Del Mar. You do like Southwest cuisine, don't you?"

"Love it." She nudged him playfully. "And it's got to be better than boxed macaroni."

"You can say that again."

Twenty minutes later, they entered the small stucco café and were shown through the dusky candlelight to a small table in a private corner. Surrounding the simple wicker furnishings were huge colorful clay pots with cactus and palm fronds. Completing the south-of-the-border decor were Aztec-style stone fountains and colorful wall hangings portraying California missions.

After they were seated and given menus, Frannie leaned across the table and whispered, "The atmosphere here is wonderful! Why didn't we come here weeks ago?"

A sardonic smile flickered on his lips. "I was your hired model. I wasn't sure you wanted to mix business and pleasure."

She flicked her menu at him. "Scott Winslow, you're a big tease!"

"And you love it!"

She grinned. "I guess I do."

He opened his menu. "So what are you having?"

She scanned the menu items and the prices. "Scott, this place is a little pricey. I can help with the tab, if you —"

"No, this is my treat. Order whatever you like."

When the waitress came, Frannie ordered the *camarones al pescadore* — breaded shrimp, wrapped in bacon and sautéed. Scott chose the *carne asada,* with rice, beans and guacamole.

While waiting for their order, they helped themselves to warm tortilla chips and fresh salsa. As they chatted about inconsequential things, Frannie found that she couldn't take her eyes off Scott. The candlelight did amazing things to his ruggedly handsome face. And her stomach did somersaults over the way his eyes danced when he smiled at her.

After their meals had been served, Scott reached across the table and touched her hand. "I'll say grace this time, Frannie."

"All right. That would be nice."

As they bowed their heads, he took both her hands in his and offered a simple, earnest prayer.

The warm, fuzzy feeling that had started in Frannie's midriff was spreading to her heart and extremities. She liked being here with Scott, liked the way he spoke her name and the way his eyes moved over her with silent approval. Was she falling in love with him? She had suspected some days ago. The answer appeared to be a resounding yes.

And yet, how could she love him when she still knew so little about him?

He leaned across and table and said confidentially, "A penny for your thoughts."

She smiled. "Oh, it'll cost you more than that."

"How about an I.O.U.?"

"Deal. I was just thinking how much fun this is. I hope we can do it again."

"I don't see why not."

She poked idly at her shrimp. "Scott, I hope you don't mind my saying this, but I feel as if I'm seeing you in a whole new light."

"How so?"

"I don't know if I can explain it."

"I'm no longer the crazy drifter on the beach?"

"That's part of it. I don't want this to sound off the wall, but I feel a connection between us. As if we're kindred spirits. Soul mates somehow. Even though I don't know much about your past, in some ways I feel as if I know you better than anyone I've ever met. Does that sound bizarre?"

"No, Frannie." He clasped her hand in his. "I feel as if I know you, too. I know your heart, and it's pure and sincere and beautiful. I've never known a woman like you."

"You sound like you've known a lot of women."

"I've had my fair share of relationships, but they never worked out. When I moved into the beach house, I resolved to keep my distance from all women. Permanently. Then you came pounding on my door." He lifted her hand to his mouth and kissed her fingertips. "Now, dear Frannie, you've got my head spinning. I don't know what to think."

Her voice escaped in a baffled whisper. "Neither do I, Scott." Did she dare tell him she felt as bedazzled as he?

Chapter Ten

Almost unnoticed, September had settled in with a relentless shimmering heat. Frannie was caught unawares. Where had the time gone since she had moved here to her beach bungalow? How could summer be over and autumn already in the wings?

For two weeks now Frannie and Scott had been meeting every day for devotions on the beach. At midmorning, after a brisk run with Ruggs, they would spread out a blanket on the sand and put a praise tape in her boom box. Then they would sit together under the blazing sun and take turns reading aloud from the letters of the apostle Paul.

Often, Scott would interrupt the reading to insert a comment or a question — "What do you think Paul meant by this? . . . This Paul was quite an opinionated guy. . . . Hey, he could have been writing about our world today."

When they had finished reading the Bible and discussing the verses, they would hold hands and take turns praying. At first, their prayers were brief and a bit self-conscious, with awkward pauses and a fumbling for words. But then something happened. One day Frannie noticed that their prayers had become earnest and impassioned. They were no longer aware of the time. And most important, she felt a closeness with God she hadn't felt before.

These devotional times that had begun almost out of a sense of duty had now become the most important part of her day. Not only was she cultivating a closer relationship with God, but she and Scott were developing a closeness she hadn't anticipated, as well. Other than occasional prayers with her father, Frannie had never revealed her spiritual side to another person, and certainly not to a handsome young drifter on the beach.

Today, Frannie found herself waking at dawn and counting the hours until her special time with Scott. Nothing else seemed as important, not even her work. She hadn't started a new sculpture since finishing the soldier, even though she had a new commission for the bust of a child. To her consternation, if she wasn't sculpting

Scott, her heart wasn't in it.

As she showered and dressed in a sleeveless blouse and cutoffs, she mused that she had never experienced a friendship like Scott's. He not only nurtured her emotions and her spirit, but his very touch was electrifying.

Now, as she and Ruggs crossed the beach to their usual morning rendezvous, she told herself that she couldn't be in love with this man, even though her heart told her she was. Surely he was just a friend, a cherished confidant during this changing phase of her life. They were good for each other on a temporary basis. As she helped nurture his budding spirituality, he was helping her regain a passion for her faith and a hunger for God's presence in her everyday life. They had both been careful not to mention anything that would suggest a more permanent relationship.

No matter how much Frannie cared about Scott, she had to remember that he was a man without a past or a future. He had made that clear to her often enough. He refused to divulge any details of his personal history just as he avoided speculating about the future — his or theirs. They shared these present, fleeting days of summer, and that had to be enough.

Accept him as he is, Frannie. Don't ask questions. Just enjoy his company for as long as it lasts. She gave herself this little pep talk every day as she walked across the beach to their special meeting place. She reminded herself that she had to be on her guard and keep her emotions in check. Otherwise, when Scott greeted her with a friendly embrace, she would imagine him smothering her with kisses and be swept up in a delirium of bliss. And that would spoil everything.

Today she found Scott already ensconced on the blanket, reading his Bible. Ruggs bounded over to him and licked his face.

With a bemused laugh, Frannie sat down cross-legged beside him. "You can see how much Ruggs has missed you. He can't stop kissing your whole face."

Scott gave the panting dog a playful hammerlock and rumpled his fur. "What about his master? Did she miss me?"

"Not that much."

Scott winked. "Too bad."

Frannie elbowed him. "Don't get smart, mister."

Scott released the dog and sent a broken shell skittering over the sand. "Go get it, boy!"

They both laughed as Ruggs scrambled

after the shell. Frannie rose up on one knee. "Are you ready for our jog?"

"Let's jog later, okay? I'm reading some good verses here."

Frannie sat back down and peered over his shoulder at the open book. "Which ones?"

"The first letter to the Corinthians. Chapter thirteen."

"Oh, the love chapter. That's a beauty."

"It says there's faith, hope and love, but the greatest of these is love."

"Yes, everything else is pretty empty without love."

Scott gave her a long, scrutinizing look. "Do you really believe that?"

"Yes, the Bible says it. It must be so."

"Do you think it's talking just about our love for God? And His love for us?"

"Partly. The Great Commandment says we should love God with all our heart, mind, soul and strength. I don't know if any of us really try to do that. We would have to galvanize all our senses, our thoughts, our emotions, and our energy to love God that way."

Scott nodded. "Yeah, I've got a long way to go on that one."

"It also says we should love one another as we love ourselves. That's a hard one to manage, too."

"It's not something we can do by ourselves."

"True. We can love like that only when God fills us with His love."

Scott's eyes moved over her with an odd expression, as if he were debating whether to say something more, and then thought better of it.

"Something on your mind, Scott?"

"No, just pondering these concepts. Trying to decide how they fit in with everyday life."

"Your life?"

His jaw tightened. "Maybe."

She searched his dusky eyes, her courage growing. "Scott, can't you trust me enough to tell me who you are?"

A guarded smile twisted his lips. "You know who I am. Scott Winslow, your number one rescuer."

"I need more than that, Scott. Why won't you tell me?"

He closed the Bible and set it on the blanket, his troubled eyes avoiding hers. "You know everything you need to know about me, Frannie. You know the person I am today. Anything else is irrelevant."

"Not to me. I can't help feeling there must be something terrible in your past to keep you so secretive, even after all these weeks when we've become so close."

He twisted a corner of the flannel blanket into a jagged snake. "I never deliberately hurt anyone, but I made many mistakes that caused people pain. I'm not proud of my past. I don't want to talk about it, because I'm not that man anymore, and I don't want to be reminded of him."

"I understand that, Scott, but —"

"Frannie, can't you accept me as the person I am today — a simple, ordinary man who wants to live close to the earth and close to God?"

"I do accept you, Scott. But you can't live the life of a reclusive drifter forever."

"I'm not reclusive. I made friends with you, didn't I?"

"But who else, Scott? You've isolated yourself from the rest of the world. You talk about wanting to know God better, but you won't even go to church with me. And what about a real job? Are you satisfied just being a beach bum?"

He ran his hand along her arm. "Is that how you see me? As a worthless beach bum?"

"No . . . yes . . . I don't know." Tears welled in her eyes. "I care so much about you, Scott. You're sensitive, witty, intelligent and creative. But you're also totally disengaged from the real world. Don't you have any ambition for a career, a future, a home, a family?"

He was silent for several minutes as he moved his palm idly over the sand, forming little ridges beside the blanket.

Frannie wondered if he had withdrawn so far into himself that he had forgotten she was there. Had she pushed too hard, gone too far? Would he close her out forever now?

Finally he looked at her. Something had shifted in his face. It was as if the mask had dropped, revealing a naked, raw vulnerability. "Do you know, Frannie, what it's like to be trapped in a life you can't change? To be riddled with guilt? To feel your life isn't your own?"

"I suppose I don't."

"Because every detail of your existence has been orchestrated by powers beyond your control? Do you know what it's like to feel disgusted with yourself, because you've allowed others to define who and what you are? You're repulsed by the person you've become, but you're too weak to do anything about it."

"That would be very painful."

Scott continued, his voice solemn, fervent. "I wasn't just making conversation when I said I've hungered all my adult life for spiritual fulfillment, for something to explain and justify my existence in this world. I had to cut every tie to the past to be strong enough to make that search. Now I'm finding the answers I need. You've helped me, Frannie. You've helped me find the God of my childhood, a faith I thought had been snuffed out years ago. I know someday I have to make my peace with the past. But not until I know I'm strong enough to hold on to the person I'm becoming . . . a man of conviction and integrity. Do you understand, Frannie? Does any of this make sense to you?"

She moved closer and placed her hand on his arm. "In a strange way, I do understand. And if you're asking me to have faith in you, I do. I won't ask any more questions until you're ready to tell me."

He slipped his arm around her shoulder and she nestled her head against his sturdy chest. She could feel his pounding heart through his tank top and smell the suntan lotion on his warm skin. They sat like that, pensive and silent, until Ruggs came leaping back with the shell in his mouth.

They both laughed as Scott wrestled with the playful canine and pretended to grab for the shell. Finally Ruggs dropped it on the ground and waited, tail wagging, for Scott to throw it again. Frannie watched the two interact, her heart swelling with affection for this intriguing man with the mysterious past. Someday he would open up to her, and whatever he was hiding, it wouldn't change how she felt about him.

Scott looked at her, his eyes crinkling merrily. "Guess we'd better get back to our study."

She chuckled. "If Ruggs will let us."

"Oh, he'll let us. Come here, boy!" Scott pulled Ruggs down beside him on the blanket and kneaded his ears. "Watch, he'll be in a trance before we know it."

By the time they had finished their devotions, Ruggs was snoozing beside them, his legs twitching as he dreamed.

Frannie hoisted herself up and brushed the sand from her bare legs. "Time for our jog, but I hate to wake Ruggs."

Scott stood, too. "Let him sleep. We won't be gone long."

"Are you sure? I never let him outside alone."

"He'll be fine. He can catch up with us. But my guess is he'll still be sawing logs when we get back."

Frannie gave her pet a lingering glance. "I guess you're right. I must sound like an overprotective mother."

Scott fingered a strand of her flyaway hair. "It becomes you. Ready to go?"

"You bet. Better watch out. I'll leave you in the dust."

"Not a chance. I'm in top form today."

"You say that every day!"

"And every day I win."

"Not today!"

They broke into a run and raced side by side for nearly twenty minutes, neither speaking. When they reached their usual spot, a balmy palm tree beside a rocky bluff, they stopped and collapsed on the sand, shoulder to shoulder, both gasping for breath. Scott gave her a sidelong glance, his chest heaving. "I won."

"I did!"

"Okay, it was a tie."

"Poor sport!" Frannie licked her dry lips. "Can't stand to have a woman beat you."

Scott leaned up on one elbow and looked at her. "You can beat me any day you please. But you've got to do it fair and square."

"I did!"

"Did not!"

She gazed at him, savoring his closeness and the way his dark eyes crinkled and his tanned face glistened under the hot sun. They exchanged companionable smiles.

"What are you thinking?" she asked.

He twined a lock of her hair around his finger. "Nothing much. Just noticing how beautiful you are with the sun's healthy glow on your skin."

She laughed. "You mean, I'm perspiring."

"I didn't say that. I'm saying I like what I see."

She lifted her fingers to his stubbled chin. "So do I."

He bent his face to hers and lightly kissed her lips, then looked at her as if to say, Do you mind? Before she could utter a reply, his mouth came down on hers with a firmness that stole her breath. The kiss deepened as he gathered her into his arms and held her close. The moment was everything she had imagined it to be, and more. She wound her arms around him and returned the kiss, her senses igniting like fireworks.

Frannie lost track of time in his arms.

When she heard the distant sound of a dog barking, she rallied and looked up at Scott. "How long have we been here?"

He kissed the top of her head and tightened his embrace. "I don't know. Time stopped the first time I kissed you."

She pulled away and sat at attention. "That dog barking. Could it be Ruggs?"

"I don't think so. We wouldn't hear Ruggs from here. Besides, he's probably still dozing."

"Still, we'd better get back." She jumped up too fast and felt a lightness in her head. She swayed, her knees buckling.

Scott sprang to his feet and caught her. "You okay?"

"Too much sun."

"Or too many kisses?"

She leaned into him. "Never too many kisses."

He slipped his arm around her waist. "You've had enough running. We'd better walk back."

What had been a twenty-minute jog became a forty-minute walk back up the beach. Frannie had butterflies in her stomach. She couldn't be sure whether they were the result of too much sun, jogging without eating or being dazzled by Scott's closeness.

When they reached the blanket, the Bible and boom box were still there. But not Ruggs.

Frannie looked around. "Where is he?"

Scott gathered up their belongings. "He probably wandered back up to the house."

Frannie ran across the sand to her beach house and searched the yard. She put her hands to her mouth and shouted Ruggs's name. She was met with only a deafening silence. "He's not here, Scott. Where could he have gone?"

"Maybe to my place." He put their gear on the porch. "Let's go."

As they ran along the beach, they took turns calling for Ruggs. They searched the area around Scott's bungalow, but again, no sign of the shaggy dog.

"Scott, do you think someone took him?"

"I don't know. Our stuff was still there on the blanket, untouched. Doesn't seem likely someone would come by and snatch a pet."

"Then where is he?" Hysteria was edging Frannie's voice.

Scott gripped Frannie's shoulders. "Listen, why don't you go back to your house and wait there? Ruggs may have wandered off or come looking for us. He'll probably come home anytime now. Meanwhile, I'll keep looking for him."

"You'd do that?" Tears glistened in her eyes. "You'd spend your day looking for my dog?"

He touched the corner of her lips. "I'd do just about anything to make you smile again."

Frannie returned to her bungalow and busied herself in her kitchenette, scouring the countertops. Then she rearranged the magazines and junk mail on the small desk in her living room. Between tasks, she stared out the windows, first one window, then another, watching for Ruggs. She couldn't concentrate on anything except the fact that she had somehow lost her precious pet, the animal that had been with her since before her mother died.

She had suffered enough casualties. Ruggs was a loss she simply could not tolerate. He was her dependable companion, the one constant in her life these days, other than Scott and her revived faith. Surely now that she felt close to God again, He wouldn't hurt her by taking Ruggs away.

For the umpteenth time she stared out the front window. "Lord, please bring Ruggs home to me. I'm sorry I let my love for You grow cold after Mama died. I'm sorry I resented You for taking her away. I'm sorry I disappointed Daddy by moving out when Juliana and Belina moved in. I'll do anything You ask if You'll just let Ruggs be okay."

Later that afternoon Scott arrived at her door, solemn-faced and empty-handed. "I'm sorry, Frannie. I couldn't find him." He held out his arms to her. "I searched every inch of this beach for a mile in both directions."

She sank against him and covered her

mouth to stifle a sob.

"But I'm not through looking. I'm taking the car out and checking the streets beyond the beach, outside our neighborhood."

"You think he ran away? That he's wandering some street somewhere?"

"There's a chance. When he awoke and we weren't there, he might have gone looking for us and gotten lost."

"He's not used to being out alone."

He held her at arm's length. "Do you want to go with me?"

"Absolutely!" She hurried to the bedroom, grabbed her purse and followed him out the door.

They drove up and down every street within two miles of her beach house. Scott drove slowly, keeping his eye on traffic, while Frannie scanned the roadsides. For an hour they drove, retracing the streets closest to home, going up and down boulevards so that Frannie could search both sides.

The sun was setting in a brilliant red sky, the daylight waning, and still no sign of her cherished pet.

A knot tightened in Frannie's chest. "He's gone, isn't he, Scott? I'm not going to find him."

"We'll keep driving as long as we have enough light."

"What then? We just go home and forget about him?"

"We pray that he's waiting for us on the porch."

Frannie breathed the words, "Please, God, let it be!"

Scott sat forward, suddenly alert, his hands gripping the steering wheel. "What's that, Frannie? There, by the side of the road." He slowed the vehicle to a crawl, and they both stared at the furry mound beside the curb.

Frannie gasped, her stomach clenching, a sour taste rising in her throat. "No, Scott, no! It can't be Ruggs! Please don't let it be Ruggs!"

Chapter Eleven

"Frannie, it's Ruggs!" Scott was down on one knee, examining the stricken animal.

She got out of the car and approached, covering her mouth lest the nauseous spasm in her stomach turn to retching. "I can't bear to look. Is he dead, Scott?"

"No, Frannie. He's still alive!"

She stooped down over the wounded dog and touched his matted fur. He was panting hard and made no effort to raise his head. "He's hurt bad, isn't he?"

"Looks that way. A car must have hit him and kept going. Let's get him to the animal hospital."

"Scott, it's a good ten miles from here."

"Then let's go. We have no time to waste." Scott gathered the limp dog up in his arms and placed him in the back seat of his car.

As Scott drove, Frannie reached into the

back seat and stroked Ruggs's ears. He made a high-pitched moaning sound and tried to wag his tail. Frannie kept up a steady stream of conversation, her voice shrill, tremulous. "You'll be okay, boy. Just hold on! You're a good dog. Don't die, Ruggsy. Please don't die!"

The drive seemed to take forever, even though the dashboard clock told her it was less than twenty minutes. Scott pulled into the first parking spot, threw open the car door, scooped Ruggs up and carried him inside.

"We need some help here!" he called to an attendant in the modest waiting room. The wiry man dashed to Scott's aid and helped carry the burly animal into an examination room.

Frannie started to follow, but the receptionist at the desk — a stout woman with cropped brown hair — called Frannie back. "Sit down, miss. The doctor will be out shortly."

Frannie started to protest, then sank down wearily in a straight-back chair. Her knees were shaking, her arms shivering — a case of nerves and the frigid air-conditioning. She was still dressed in her cutoffs and sleeveless blouse.

After a minute, Scott came out, his shirt

smeared with blood, his expression inscrutable. "The doctor's checking him over. He'll give us his diagnosis as soon as he can. I'm going to go wash up. Be right back."

She nodded and turned her gaze back to the closed door. Ruggs was in there, hurt and bleeding, maybe dying. She should insist that they let her in. She needed to be with her pet, comforting him. If she held him, maybe he wouldn't be afraid.

Scott returned and sat down beside her. He took her cold hand in his warm one. His eyes were shadowed with concern. "You okay?"

She nodded, not trusting herself to speak.

He slipped his arm around her shoulder and pulled her against him. "Ruggs is going to make it, Frannie. We've prayed for him all day. God can take care of him."

She sniffled. "I know God can, but that doesn't mean He will."

Scott nuzzled her hair. "We've got to trust Him to do what's best for us, Frannie, even if we don't understand it. You're the one who taught me that."

She brushed away a tear. "Every time I start trusting God again, He takes someone or something I love away from me. How can I believe He really loves me?"

"Well, you convinced me. You helped me

see that God doesn't promise us a perfect life, but He promises to see us through the hard times. You said it yourself. He'll never forsake us, no matter what."

She smiled up at him through a blur of tears. "I did teach you well, didn't I?"

He squeezed her arm. "I couldn't have asked for a better mentor."

"I talk a good fight but don't do so well in the heat of battle."

"You're doing fine, sweetheart. Just keep hanging in there."

"I'm trying, but I feel so weak right now. I hate being such a wimp."

"You're the cutest wimp I ever saw." He massaged her shoulder. "Seriously, you're stronger than you think you are. Remember what Paul said, 'When I am weak, then I am strong.' "

"I know. When we give God our weaknesses, He turns them into His strength. I just don't know how to give them to Him."

"We start by asking." Scott bent his lips to her ear and whispered a prayer for healing for Ruggs and strength for Frannie.

When he had finished, she lifted her face to his. Even in the fluorescent glare of this spartan office, he looked wonderful — his dark eyes full of sympathy, his full lips arced in a smile. No wonder she was falling in love with this man. He made her feel cherished and protected. No man, except her father, had made her feel that way before.

"A penny for your thoughts," he murmured.

She managed a smile. "They're worth much more than a penny."

"How about a million dollars?"

She ran her fingers over the stubble on his cleft chin. "I'll tell you one of these days . . . when the time is right."

"I'll hold you to that promise."

A deep, thickly accented voice interrupted. "Miss Rowlands?"

Frannie looked up into the face of a bald, portly man in a lab coat, a clipboard under his arm.

"I am Dr. Augustino." He pulled a chair over and sat down, facing her, his shaggy brows crouching over black, bespectacled eyes. "I have finished my examination."

Frannie sat forward, all her senses alert. "Will Ruggs be okay?"

Dr. Augustino drummed his fingers on the clipboard. "Your dog was apparently struck by an automobile. He needs surgery to repair a broken leg and a fractured hip. With your permission, we will operate tonight. Barring any complications, he should make a full recovery."

Frannie sank back in her chair and folded her hands under her chin. “Praise God!”

“If you agree to the surgery, Miss Rowlands, you will need to sign these papers.”

“I will. Just tell me when Ruggs will be able to come home.”

“In a few days. Again, assuming he responds well to the surgery.”

Her fingers stiffened. “Is there a chance he wouldn’t do well?”

“There are no guarantees, of course. But I anticipate no problems. You may go home, if you wish, and we will call you.”

“No, Doctor,” Scott replied. “We’ll wait here until Ruggs comes out of surgery.”

“Very well. It will take some time. You may wait in the consultation room. The couch there is more comfortable than these chairs.”

Frannie held out her hand for the clipboard. “Thank you, Dr. Augustino. I’ll sign those papers now.”

Afterward, the receptionist led them to a cozy room with an overstuffed sofa, armchairs and end tables with bell jar lamps.

“A little touch of home,” Scott mused as they settled on the couch. He slipped his arm around her. “Put your feet up, Frannie, and catch a few winks, if you like.”

She nestled her head in the crook of his

arm. "I'll put my feet up, but I can't sleep. Not when I'm so worried about Ruggs."

"He'll be fine. The doc says so."

"He has to be okay. This never would have happened if I hadn't taken him away from home. He always had a fenced yard. We never let him out on the street, except on a leash."

"It's not your fault, Frannie. Don't blame yourself."

"But it is my fault. I got so caught up in my own freedom, I didn't see the danger in letting Ruggs be free, too. All because I wanted to get away from home." Her hand flew to her mouth. "Oh, Scott, I just remembered. I should phone my dad and sisters. They need to know what happened."

"Let's wait until after the surgery. Then you can give them the good news."

"You're right. We'll wait." She rested her palm on his arm. "Thanks for being here with me. I couldn't have gone through this alone."

He lifted her face to his, his eyes searching hers. "I'll always be here for you, Frannie, for as long as you want."

A shiver of excitement danced along her spine. "What if I say . . . forever?"

"Forever's a long time. You'd get tired of me."

"No, I wouldn't. I'd never stop learning fascinating things about you. It would be a wonderful adventure."

Scott flinched, and a shadow crossed his face. Frannie couldn't be sure, but she had a feeling he was withdrawing from her in some secret way she couldn't comprehend.

She studied his solemn face. "Did I say something wrong?"

"No. What makes you think that? I just . . ." His voice trailed off.

"What is it, Scott? Am I reading the signals wrong? These past few weeks, you've made me believe there's something special going on between us. And then today, when you kissed me . . . that wasn't the kiss of a casual friend."

"I know. I let my guard down, Frannie. I shouldn't have. It's not fair to you."

She bristled. "Not fair? What do you mean?"

"I can't explain it. It's just that I would never want to hurt you. You mean more to me than anyone."

"And you mean the world to me, Scott."

He pulled her closer. "If I could, I would keep our lives exactly as they are today — the two of us living in our beach bungalows and shutting out the rest of the world. In my dreams, I even imagine a little bungalow for two. Just you and me, Frannie. And Ruggs, of course."

"That's a beautiful dream, Scott."

"But it's only that. A dream. I can't turn it into reality."

"You can't?" A sliver of hurt pricked her heart. "Why not, Scott? What aren't you telling me?"

His eyes grew distant, clouded. He had slipped away to some other place, a world he still refused to divulge to her.

"Scott, why can't you talk about the past? I know it haunts your every waking hour. Please tell me. How can our relationship go to the next level if you don't let me see who you were before you came here?"

His voice took on a defensive edge. "And what if that man isn't the person you think you know?"

"Whoever you were before isn't as important as the man you are today. But I want to care about the whole man, not just facets you choose to reveal. I want to know your history, your heritage, all the experiences that make you the man you are."

"Are you so eager for the truth that you'd risk destroying what we have together?"

An icy chill swept over her. "Are you saying I wouldn't want to be with you if I knew the truth?"

"I didn't say that. It's just that my life is — *was* — very complicated. And once the genie is uncorked from the bottle, you can't get him back inside. Everything changes. Everything reverts. The fantasy is gone, and I'm back to reality."

"You're not making any sense, Scott. You keep talking in riddles, metaphors."

"Because I'm trying to protect what we have here, Frannie, this beautiful, delicate thing, whatever it is, between us."

"So am I, Scott. That's why I need you to be honest with me."

"Honesty, huh? Remember what happened to Eve in the garden of Eden?" His voice took on a bantering tone, but she knew it was just another delaying tactic. "Eve was determined to eat from the tree of knowledge, to learn the difference between good and evil. And look what happened to her. She ended up with a snake in the grass."

"That's not funny, Scott."

"I'm not trying to be funny. I just don't want to lose you, Frannie. We can't change the past or predict the future. All we have is today, and no one knows how long it will last."

"God knows."

"Yes, He does. I just pray He's not telling

us it's over already."

Shivering, she folded her arms across her chest. "You scare me when you talk like that."

"You wanted honesty. I'm being honest. I'm on borrowed time, Frannie. Delaying the inevitable. One day I'll be sucked back into the vortex of my past, and the Scott Winslow you know will cease to exist. And, believe me, you won't like the person in his place."

"Stop it, Scott. I won't listen —"

"I'm just saying, midnight will come. You'll turn into a pumpkin, and I'll turn into a rat. So much for fairy tales and 'happily ever after.' Is that the truth you want to hear?"

In a small, hushed voice she asked, "Are you telling me you're married?"

He heaved a careworn sigh. "No, I'm not married. How can you even ask that? If I were, I wouldn't have allowed things to progress the way they have between us."

"Then whatever your problems are, we can deal with them together, Scott. Please, let me help you."

He released her and shifted so that they were no longer touching. "There's nothing you can do, Frannie. I have enough entanglements to sink even an honorable man in the mire. I won't bog you down with my troubles. You don't deserve it."

"I don't deserve this, Scott." Tears pressed behind her eyes. "I'm worried sick about Ruggs. I can't deal with anything else tonight. And now, when I most need your comfort, you insinuate all these horrible things and make me doubt you. Make me doubt *us!*"

"I'm sorry, baby." He gathered her back into his arms and kissed her forehead, her cheeks, her lashes. "I don't know how we got off on this tangent, sweetheart. Forget I said anything, okay? We'll keep things just the way they are. We'll make the rest of the world go away, and it'll just be the two of us for as long as you want."

Frannie nodded, reveling in Scott's warm embrace. Yes, God willing, it would be just the two of them, forever.

But a shadow of doubt lingered. How long could she and Scott keep the rest of the world at bay? And what dark secret from his past threatened their happiness, their future?

Chapter Twelve

Ruggs was coming home today. After three days of recuperation, he was ready to be released from the animal hospital. Scott had suggested that he and Frannie go together to pick up her recovering pet and bring him home.

But that wasn't what had Frannie's anxiety level hitting the ceiling. It was the anticipation of being with Scott. Several times over the past few days, he had insinuated that tonight would be more than just Ruggs's homecoming. He had all but admitted that he would divulge the secrets that had shrouded their communication from the beginning.

Just last night he had said, "I think I'm finally strong enough to face the ghosts of my past. Once we have Ruggs settled back at home, maybe we can talk. You need to know everything. We can't begin to plan our future until we've made peace with the past."

His words echoed in her mind all last night and all day today, igniting her hopes and coloring her dreams.

Now Scott was due to arrive at any moment.

Frannie couldn't contain her excitement. She paced the floor of her beach house, watching out the window and stealing glances in the mirror at her sleeveless shell top and white stretch jeans. For once, she liked what she saw. Usually she wore her long blond hair straight, with a carefree, unattended look. But today she had taken her curling iron and coaxed her silky locks into luxuriant, cascading curls.

Surely Scott would approve. She could almost picture the look of delight on his face as his umber-brown eyes swept over her. Time and again today she had mentally rehearsed their conversation. She heard herself confessing to Scott that she was in love with him. Surely he suspected, but she had never actually said the words. She was convinced he loved her, too, and wanted to tell her so . . . except for that dark chapter of his life that held him back.

Perhaps it was more than a chapter. An entire book perhaps. But whatever it was, surely, with God's help, they could deal with it and pave the way for a future together. After all, knowledge was power. It was not knowing the truth that undermined their closeness. But tonight everything would be disclosed and there would be no more secrets between them.

Frannie heard a car in the driveway. She slipped on her sandals, grabbed her clutch purse and flung open the door with a cheerful "Scott, you're right on time!"

But it wasn't Scott. A tall, statuesque woman stood on the porch in a rust-red blouse and matching herringbone skirt and jacket. Her red hair was swept up in a twist and her makeup was dramatic and flawless. She couldn't have been more than twenty-five, even though she exuded an aura of jaded sophistication.

"I'm sorry," Frannie blurted. "I thought you were someone else."

"Obviously." The woman's voice was heavy with sarcasm.

An alarm went off somewhere in Frannie's mind. "May I help you?"

"Yes, but he's obviously not here."

"Who?"

"Scott. Scott Winslow. He is the man you thought you were greeting at the door, is he not?"

Frannie hesitated, then conceded, "Yes. I'm expecting him at any moment."

The woman gazed around curiously. "Then he doesn't live here in this dreary little cabin?"

Frannie swallowed her rising indignation. "No, he certainly doesn't. Are you a friend of Scott's?"

A Mona Lisa smile flickered on the woman's full crimson lips. "Yes, you could say that."

"Well, if you'll give me your name, I'll tell him you stopped by."

The woman's cool sea-green eyes drilled into Frannie's, unnerving her. "May I come in and wait?"

"I'm not sure that's a good idea. If you'll just leave your name —"

"He hasn't told you about me, has he?"

Frannie managed to keep her voice steady. "That depends on who you are."

"I'm Vivian LaVelle. Does that ring any bells?"

"No, it doesn't. But I'd be glad to give Scott a message for you."

The woman scowled. "You can do better than that. You can tell me which scummy, decrepit little cabin he lives in on this asinine beach. And don't tell me he doesn't live here. My sources have reported that he's here, living like a foolish, eccentric hermit."

Frannie said coolly, "Why should I tell you anything about Scott?"

Vivian raised one finely plucked eyebrow. "You are a simpleton, aren't you? I bet Scott hasn't even told you who he is."

Frannie wavered. "He's told me everything I need to know."

"And haven't you wondered why a man in Scott's position would be living in a hovel on the beach?"

"Scott's position?"

"He hasn't told you, has he? What did he do, lie about his name?"

"He wouldn't lie about that. He's Scott Winslow."

"And the name means nothing to you?"

"What are you getting at, Miss LaVelle?"

"For most people, the name Scott Winslow summons images of a billion-dollar real estate empire. Or don't you read the newspapers?"

The skin prickled on the back of Frannie's neck. "Of course, I read —" The truth struck her like a fist in the stomach. She nearly doubled over. "Maybe . . . maybe you'd better come in after all, Miss LaVelle."

"I figured you'd want to hear more." The

woman stepped inside and gazed around with a detached nonchalance. "The detective I hired observed Scott in this very cottage, coming and going several times. For the life of me, I don't know what Scottie was thinking, pretending to be a common beachcomber."

"Sit down, Miss LaVelle. Please, you obviously know more about Scott than I do. Tell me everything."

In a smooth, graceful gesture, the woman sat down on the couch and crossed her long legs at the knee. "Since it appears we have something in common, call me Vivian. And you are . . . ?"

"Frances Rowlands. Frannie. A friend of Scott's."

"A good friend, by the reports I've received. If Scott doesn't live here with you, he must live in one of the other beach houses nearby."

Frannie sat down in the overstuffed chair by the fireplace. "I assure you Scott doesn't live here. But we did spend a lot of time together this past summer. I'm a sculptor. He was my model."

A brittle smile crimped Vivian's lips. "How quaint . . . and how convenient for Scott."

Frannie chose to ignore the coarse insinuation. "Tell me how you know Scott."

Vivian lifted her tapered fingers and examined a long polished nail. The color was fire-engine red. "Isn't it obvious how I know him?"

"No, it's not. You haven't told me anything you couldn't have read in the newspaper."

Vivian sat forward and glared at Frannie, her face as cold and unyielding as a painted porcelain doll's. "Then listen carefully, Miss Frances Rowlands. Scott Winslow lives in a multimillion-dollar mansion on the Santa Barbara coast. His family is one of the wealthiest in America. They own half the real estate between San Diego and San Francisco. In fact, they own this dilapidated joint you're living in, plus every other rinky-dink bungalow on this beach. They don't always play by the rules, but they are ruthless and they always win, no matter who gets hurt."

Every word Vivian spoke felt like a slap across Frannie's cheek, a dagger to her heart. She struggled to find her voice, her defenses crumbling. "The man you're describing . . . he isn't anything like the Scott Winslow I know."

"Isn't he? Did your Scott Winslow move to the beach about seven or eight months ago? Has he told you some irrational story about wanting to get back to nature and live the simple life? Has he been secretive about his past?"

"What if he has?"

"I'll tell you why." Vivian's green, thickly lashed eyes narrowed. "Last year Scott began to complain about his rich, privileged life. He joked about running away from all his responsibilities and becoming a carefree vagabond on some exotic beach. I didn't take him seriously. But apparently he wanted a taste of the humble, unadorned life before taking the big plunge."

"The big plunge?"

Vivian's crimson lips tightened against perfect, white teeth. "Scott Winslow is my fiancé. Our wedding is next month."

Frannie flinched, as stunned and disoriented as if a lightning bolt had struck between her eyes. "You're Scott's fiancée?"

"That's what I've been trying to tell you." Vivian's lips puckered in an exaggerated pout. "Obviously my naughty little Scottie wanted some time to himself — or should I say some time to play — before we get married. I'm really going to have to give him a slap on the wrist for letting me worry about him all these months. Just you wait until I get him back home!"

Frannie's head spun. This moment couldn't be real. Surely she was dreaming, trapped in the worst nightmare of her life. *Dear God, let me wake up, please!*

"You look a bit pale, Miss Rowlands, I mean, Frances. You did say that was your name, didn't you?"

"Frannie. They call me Frannie."

"Yes, of course. Now, Frannie, if you'll just tell me where I can find my roguish swain, I'll be on my way."

"He — he lives in the next cottage. Just down the beach. You can see it from here."

Vivian stood up and smoothed her expensive jacket over her shapely hips. "Thank you, Frannie. You've been very helpful. I hope my naughty Scottie didn't lead you on or fill your sweet head with sentimental nonsense. He's a very shrewd, hardheaded entrepreneur. But once in a while he gets these romantic notions that he has to rescue some damsel in distress. He's a bit like Don Quixote tilting at windmills. I have to go out and bring him back to reality. But I adore him, no matter how flawed he is. I'm sure he captivated you too. For a scoundrel, he can be disarmingly charming. Don't you agree?"

Frannie's thoughts were racing pell-mell. This had to be a terrible mistake. But it appeared that the biggest mistake was Frannie's, for trusting a mysterious man named Scott Winslow.

"Since it doesn't appear that Scott is coming here, I will go to him. You said the next beach house?"

"Yes. You can get there by the beach, if you don't mind walking. Or you can go back out to the street and drive down. It's about a quarter mile."

"I'll drive. Thank you, Miss Rowlands. You've been very helpful."

In a daze Frannie escorted the woman outside to the porch and stood watching numbly as she strutted out to her vehicle, a foreign red convertible. With a haughty nod in Frannie's direction, she climbed in, backed out of the driveway and headed down the street in the direction of Scott's house.

What just happened here? Frannie asked herself as she went back inside and shut the door. Who was this woman? Was she a crackpot, a deranged troublemaker, a stalker? Perhaps everything she had told Frannie was a lie. Why did I let her in my house? Why did I even admit I knew Scott? Why did I tell her where he lives?

There was no way to phone Scott and warn him. And what if the woman wasn't lying? What if she actually was Scott's fiancée? Frannie sat down at her small kitchen table and massaged her knuckles. What should she do now? Run the length of the beach to Scott's house to see what kind of reception he gave this bizarre woman, Vivian LaVelle?

Frannie stood up and went to the window. "Where are you, Scott?" she said aloud, her voice sounding hollow in the empty room. "You were supposed to be here by now. We're supposed to pick up Ruggs. Don't you remember?"

She had to do something, had to make a decision. Go pick up Ruggs by herself, or drive over to Scott's to see what was keeping him, or take the twenty-minute walk along the beach to Scott's bungalow and size things up, unnoticed. She decided against driving over, lest she encounter the lady LaVelle at his door. Better to go by way of the beach, a more private and circuitous route.

She went to the phone and dialed her home number. After several rings, her father answered. "Daddy, it's me, Frannie," she said, a nervous tremor in her voice. "Listen, Daddy, I was supposed to pick up Ruggs at the animal hospital, but something came up. Would you mind getting him and taking him back to your house? . . . Thanks, Daddy. I'll come by in the morning and get him . . . No, Daddy, I can't explain it right now. But I'll tell you everything when I see you."

She hung up the phone, went to the bedroom, kicked off her sandals and slipped on her sneakers. She grabbed a lightweight sweater, tossed it around her shoulders and headed outside. It was dusk now, and the ocean air was cooling quickly as the crimson sun lowered, hugging the horizon.

What am I doing? Frannie asked herself as she tramped across the beach toward Scott's cabin. I should have stayed home and waited for him to come to me. I'm going to feel like a fool if I arrive at his door and he's with this strange woman, his supposed fiancée. *Please, God, just let it be a big misunderstanding. Don't let that rude woman be the one Scott loves.*

She quickened her pace, her rubber-soled sneakers scudding over the hard-packed sand. Maybe Scott would be at home and greet her as if nothing had happened. Maybe he would have some perfectly good explanation about the nauseating, abrasive Miss LaVelle. She was someone I once knew, and she went off the deep end and got the wrong idea about us. She won't listen to reason, but just ignore her. She's no one really, she doesn't matter. . . .

By the time Frannie arrived at Scott's bungalow, the salmon-pink sky had given way to deep streamers of blue. The last faint rays of sunlight had been swallowed by ever-widening shadows. There were no lights on inside.

Frannie knocked anyway — once, twice, three times. Then, impulsively she tried the door. To her surprise, it opened. She peeked inside and called Scott's name. There was no reply. Gingerly she stepped inside and turned on the wall switch. The room was flooded with light. She looked around, blinking against the brightness.

No one was home.

A chill shot through her. She shouldn't be here checking up on Scott. She felt like an intruder, trespassing where she didn't belong. But something didn't feel right. What if Scott needed her? She called his name again as she walked down the shadowed hall to the bedroom. Her heart raced as she entered and flipped the switch. Everything was in disarray — drawers pulled out, the closet door open, toiletries and clothing on the floor and bed.

Frannie's breath caught as she looked in the closet. Most of Scott's clothes were gone. And his shoes. And luggage. Some of the drawers had been emptied, others had been left untouched. He had obviously packed in a hurry. Had he been that eager to get back to the life he had left behind?

"No!" Frannie covered her mouth with her hand. Tears stung her eyes. "He wouldn't leave like this without saying goodbye!" She ran to the door and looked out at the driveway. Scott's vintage car was still there. That meant one thing, one terrible, indisputable fact. Without a parting word or a backward glance, Scott had gone off with the woman who claimed to be his fiancée, the brassy, outrageous Vivian LaVelle.

Chapter Thirteen

For a mellow, unassuming minister of the Gospel, Andrew Rowlands's life was getting increasingly complicated. Just when he had finally adapted himself to the household routine of his lovely new bride and his taciturn stepdaughter, his youngest offspring had moved back in with a broken heart and a lame dog.

For several days after her return, Frannie wouldn't say a word about what was troubling her. But Andrew could see in her eyes how much she was hurting, and he knew the source of her pain had to be that beach bum Scott Winslow. Andrew could only imagine the loathsome things that man might have done. He hadn't trusted the evasive drifter from the beginning. There were too many unanswered questions, too many glaring gaps in his background.

Andrew should have been more forceful

in warning Frannie about him. But, for a change, he had resisted the impulse to meddle. After all, he had already batted zero in trying to set Frannie up with Wesley Hopkins, the new minister of music.

But to his own astonishment, Andrew had inadvertently achieved another matchmaking coup, pairing Wesley with his bashful Belina. The two were quite an item these days. Wesley had even persuaded Belina to start singing in the church choir, and Andrew had a feeling Wesley would even have her doing solos one of these days.

Now if Andrew could just help his youngest daughter find the man of her dreams . . . but it certainly wouldn't be the likes of Scott Winslow! The contemptible cad even had the nerve to keep phoning Frannie on both her cell phone and at Andrew's house. But at least his daughter had the good sense to refuse to speak to the man.

On the morning of Frannie's fourth day at home, as Andrew and his daughter lingered over a second cup of coffee, he seized the opportunity to question her about her plans. "Are you thinking of moving back in here for good, honey, or is this just a respite before you return to the beach house?"

"I don't know, Daddy." Frannie pushed a wisp of flaxen hair behind her ear. In spite of her tan, she looked pale and drawn and several pounds thinner. "I know I can't stay in limbo like this forever, but I honestly don't know what to do."

"If you want to come home, we can rent a truck and bring all your stuff home. I imagine you want to get back to your sculpting, and you can hardly do that with all your equipment at the beach house."

"To move home would be a step backward, Daddy, like conceding defeat. I would be admitting I can't make it on my own."

"I don't see it that way, sweetheart. You'd just be agreeing that the beach house wasn't the right choice at this time."

Frannie's eyes glistened with tears. "But I was so sure, Daddy. I was really happy there. It felt so right."

He reached across the table and covered her hand with his large palm. "Why don't you tell me what happened, honey? I know it has to do with Scott."

"I never said that."

"You didn't have to. You've refused his calls all week long. Tell me what he did to make you so unhappy."

Frannie lowered her gaze. "I didn't want you to know what a fool I've been, Daddy."

He squeezed her hand. "You know I'd

never think that. I love you, baby. You'll always be my little sunshine girl, even when your smile is turned upside down."

Frannie's lips turned up in a droll little grin. "Oh, Daddy, you always know what to say to make me feel better."

"I could do an even better job if I knew what has you so upset. What did that scoundrel do to hurt you?"

Frannie sipped her coffee. Andrew could see that something was going on — the way she blinked back tears and her chin puckered, as if she were wrestling with herself. Finally she licked her ashen lips and drew in a deep breath. "Okay, Daddy, I'll tell you." Something in her guileless tone and melancholy expression reminded him of the cherub-faced little girl who used to climb on his lap for bedtime stories.

"Take your time, honey. I've got all morning."

"It's about Scott, but you already know that."

Andrew's ire was rising. "What did he do?"

"He — he made me fall in love with him." She brushed at a tear. "I thought he loved me, too, and that we had a future together."

"What changed your mind?"

"A woman came to my door. She was

looking for Scott. I found out she's his fiancée."

Andrew sat back and rubbed his jaw. "That had to be a shock."

"There's more, Daddy." She gazed at him, her eyes glassy pools. "He's not the man I thought he was."

"I guess not — leading you on, with a fiancée in the picture!"

"That's not all of it." Frannie ran her finger over the rim of her coffee cup. Her lower lip was trembling.

Andrew winced. It hurt him to see his little girl suffering like this. "You don't have to go on, honey. I get the picture. Scott Winslow is a big-time jerk."

Frannie inhaled deeply and looked at him, her eyes filling with seething fire. "It's worse than that. Scott Winslow is a fraud, Daddy. He's not a poor beach-comber wanting to live the simple life close to nature. He's the notorious Scott Winslow with the billion-dollar real estate empire!"

Andrew sat back, startled. No, his reaction was stronger than that. He was appalled. He had been prepared to hear just about anything concerning Frannie's deceitful Lothario. But not this. "You're telling me your drifter friend is Scott

Winslow, the billionaire entrepreneur who owns half of California?"

Frannie began to weep. "Yes, Daddy. He fooled us all. He spouted all these platitudes about wanting to help the poor and make life beautiful for them. And here he's the man a judge sentenced to live in his own shabby, substandard tenement for six months. Maybe that's why Scott was living in that dilapidated beach house. The law made him!"

Andrew whistled through his teeth. "I knew the guy was hiding something, but I never dreamed his secret was this big."

"That's why I can't take his calls, Daddy. I can't bear the thought of facing him again after the fool he made of me."

Andrew pushed back his chair and went around the table. He wrapped his arms around his daughter and kissed the top of her head. "I know it hurts, honey. I'm so sorry. If there was anything I could do to make it better . . ."

She patted his arm and looked up at him with tearful eyes. "Thanks for not saying 'I told you so.' "

"Sweetheart, we're going to do everything we can to help you forget that turncoat. We've got Ruggs to nurse back to health, and I'm sure Belina will welcome your company, especially now that she's coming out of her shell."

"It's because of Wesley, isn't it? She cares about him a lot, doesn't she?"

"And the feeling seems to be mutual." Andrew massaged his daughter's shoulder. "I hope you don't regret encouraging that little romance."

"No, Daddy, I'm happy for Belina. I could never have cared about Wesley the way I . . ." As she let her words trail off, tears slid down her cheeks.

Andrew filled the awkward silence with a booming, "Come on, kiddo. Let's think of something fun to do today. Drive into San Diego and take in a play. Or go out to eat at that fabulous seafood grotto in Del Mar. Or how about the zoo? You wanna go see some silly orangutans, hippos and chimpanzees? What do you say, kid? You wanna do something crazy and fun with your ol' man?"

She managed a lopsided smile. "Shouldn't you be working on your sermon for Sunday morning?"

He waved his hand breezily. "I've got time. And right now I think my daughter needs some old-fashioned TLC. How about it?"

She gave him an appreciative hug. "Thanks, Daddy, but I'll be fine. Maybe I'll go upstairs and visit with Belina. She's probably dying to tell someone about her new romance."

"Someone her age, you mean."

Frannie nodded. "She's probably never had a girlfriend to share things with."

"Nor a sister," said Andrew meaningfully.

Frannie carried their coffee cups over to the sink, then gave Andrew a wistful smile. "Maybe Belina and I will have a chance to get closer now that I'm back home."

"I hope so, baby cakes. Just don't spend all day up there. I'm sure Juliana could use a hand in the kitchen. Don't get me wrong. She's a wonderful cook, but I'm sure she'd welcome a night off. Besides, we haven't had your spaghetti and meatballs for ages. I'll even get out the big bibs, if you like."

Frannie laughed. "Oh, Daddy, I've missed you!"

He winked at her. "And I've missed you, too, sweetheart."

After Frannie had gone upstairs, Andrew sauntered down the hall to his study and sat down at his large mahogany desk. He needed to work on his sermon notes, but he wasn't in the mood. He still couldn't reconcile the idea that the young drifter who had visited his home with Frannie was indeed the ruthless billionaire entrepreneur whose name was so often in the news. Nor could he imagine that his bright, sensitive daughter could have fallen in love with such a cold, calculating man. As elusive and puzzling as Scott Winslow had seemed that night, he seemed a thousand times more baffling and incomprehensible in light of this new information.

Andrew was scratching out a few mindless notations when the phone rang. His habit was to let someone else get it when he was working on his sermons. He waited for Juliana to pick up, then remembered that she was at the beauty parlor for her weekly hair appointment. When the girls didn't catch it on the third ring, he grabbed the receiver and said hello with exaggerated politeness, to disguise his impatience.

"Reverend Rowlands?"

The voice was familiar. Unmistakable, in fact. Andrew's outrage took over. "Scott, is that you? Scott Winslow?"

"Yes, sir. Please, don't hang up."

Andrew snapped the pencil in his hand. "You have a lot of nerve calling here after what you've done."

"I know, sir, and I'm sorry. I never intended to deceive Frannie. Or hurt her. It was the last thing I wanted to do."

"It's a little late for regrets now, don't you think? The damage is done."

"I know she hates me, but I can't let things end this way. If I could just talk to her and explain —"

"I don't think there's anything to explain," Andrew interrupted. "She doesn't want your sorry excuses. Just leave her alone, you hear me? She'll be okay."

"I can't do that. She deserves to hear the whole story."

"Do you honestly think the details of your deception will make her feel better? Give her a break, man. Make it a clean cut. Don't draw out the agony."

Desperation colored Scott's voice. "Sir, please, just tell her I called. Tell her I need to talk to her. I had to leave the cabin so quickly that night, I know I left her hanging. She must be thinking all sorts of terrible things."

"She wouldn't be thinking such terrible things if you had had the decency to tell her the truth in the first place."

"I know. I was wrong. And I need to tell her so myself."

Andrew drummed his fingers on his desk. Why was he even talking with this rapscallion? "I'll tell her you called, Scott, but I can guarantee she won't call you back."

"Reverend Rowlands, wait. Don't hang up yet. Please, listen to me. I know you're a godly, compassionate man. Would you just take down my phone number and address and tell Frannie she won't regret contacting me."

Andrew grabbed another pencil. "Go ahead, but it won't make any difference." He scribbled the information on a notepad, then said through clenched teeth, "Is that it?"

"One more thing, Reverend." A slight tremor rippled through Scott's voice. "If you believe nothing else I've said, sir, believe this."

Andrew blinked, surprised. The man sounded like he was ready to cry. "What is it, Scott?"

"I love your daughter, sir, and that's the truth."

The line went dead after that. Andrew sat for several moments replaying their conversation in his mind. The whole thing was bizarre. It made no sense. Why would a man in Scott Winslow's position care so much about a girl he had met on the beach, and betrayed? Another strange thing. Andrew didn't have the feeling that he had been talking with a cold, heartless tycoon in his lofty ivory tower. Scott Winslow had sounded like a needy, broken, remorseful human being.

Andrew raised his hands in a gesture of helplessness. “What do I do now, Lord? Throw this paper away, or tell my darling daughter this Winslow fellow may have something to say that she needs to hear?”

Chapter Fourteen

Frannie missed the beach more than she could have imagined. So did Ruggs. Now that his cast was off and his leg and hip on the mend, he was eager to romp and play in the sand again. Frannie could see it in the way he tilted his head just so and gazed dolefully at her. She nearly melted when those enormous mahogany peepers peered at her through that rag-mop of hair, as if to say, When are we going home where we belong?

It seemed strange to her that she thought of the beach house as home. But it was true. Her father's house was just a place to visit. She had been here for over two weeks now, and it was time to go before she wore out her welcome.

So on a brisk, October day with just the hint of scudding clouds on the horizon — she packed her bags, loaded her belongings into her trunk and told her father goodbye.

He and Belina walked her out to her car. She opened the passenger door and let Ruggs inside, then gave Belina a hug. "Keep me posted on how things go with Wesley, okay?"

"I will, Frannie. Thanks for listening to all my silly chatter about him. You've been a good friend."

"So have you, Belina. I'll miss you."

"I'll miss you, too. Come back soon."

Frannie's father stepped forward and gathered her into his sturdy arms. "Listen, kiddo, just because you're moving back to your beach house doesn't mean you can't come visit as often as you like."

"I know, Daddy. I'll be back soon. But right now I need some time alone to think . . . and pray."

"I'll be praying for you, too, baby doll." His eyes crinkled with a mixture of smiles and tears. "You know your ol' dad loves you."

"And I love you, Daddy. More than I can say." She lifted her face to his and kissed his cheek. "Take care of yourself."

"That goes both ways." He held the car door open for her. "Maybe I shouldn't bring up the subject, but it's been over a week now. Have you decided whether to contact Scott?"

She shrugged. "I've still got the paper with his address and phone number in my purse, but I don't know whether to call him."

"Give it time. And give it to the Lord. He'll show you what to do."

Minutes later, as Frannie drove away from her father's house, she realized this was a more painful farewell than when she first moved out. Maybe it was because she had left the first time with an innocence and expectations that had since been dashed by her disappointment in Scott.

A half hour later, Frannie pulled into the driveway beside her beach house. She could still visualize Scott's fiancée standing on the rustic porch in her expensive clothes and fancy hairdo. She pushed the image out of her mind as she carried her things into the house. Ruggs clambered in after her, still limping on his bad leg.

"Well, here we are, boy. We may be a little worse for wear, but we're home. After I get my stuff put away, we'll take a little walk on the beach and watch the sunset."

In the days that followed, Frannie made it a point to take Ruggs for a walk every evening at sunset. Sometimes weary from working on her latest commission, she would wade into the water and let the foamy waves wash over her bare legs. At other times she and Ruggs would stretch out on the sandy beach and watch the fiery sun become a crimson balloon on the deep blue horizon. She loved burrowing her toes into the warm sand while Ruggs chased a seagull or sniffed at a questionable object the waves had washed ashore.

Sometimes she brought her Bible and read or memorized verses while Ruggs dozed beside her. She loved the sense of peace and tranquillity that washed over her at moments like this. In these solitary days when she had no human support group surrounding her, God was becoming increasingly real to her. She found it easier to pray as she sat by the ocean, watching the frothy tide roll in and the sky change colors as if God were spreading his multicolored palette across the heavens.

She often talked aloud to the Lord, as if He were sitting beside her. She would pour out her heart in a blitz of words, her voice becoming one with the rushing waves, the screeching gulls, the whistling wind. But even as her spiritual life deepened, her emotions vacillated between joy and despair. On the days when her faith was strong, she released her hurt and anger to God and felt

His sweet consolation. But on other days her faith wavered and she found herself giving in to desolation.

Ten days from the day she had returned to her beach house, she received a call from Scott on her answering machine. "Frannie, I've been waiting for you to return my call. As each day passes I realize I may never hear from you again. Please give me a chance to tell my side of the story. After I've had my say, if you wish, I'll never bother you again."

Hearing Scott's voice resurrected all the painful emotions she had nearly convinced herself she no longer felt. The truth was, she still loved him, would perhaps always love him. And yet she couldn't be sure the man she loved even existed. She had fallen in love with someone that a man named Scott Winslow had carefully, deliberately manufactured. And this man — the Scott Winslow who could undertake such a cruel hoax — she hated with every fiber of her being. How could she ever again trust another man? Or even herself? How stupid and gullible was she that Scott could sweep her off her feet and convince her he was a believer like herself, compassionate and altruistic, when in reality he was a ruthless, lying fraud?

After hearing Scott's message, Frannie escaped to the beach. She walked for a long while, arguing with herself, arguing with the Lord. "What am I supposed to do? I'm caught in limbo, Lord. I can't go forward and I can't go back. I can't even concentrate on my work. All I can see is Scott's face. When I wake in the morning I think of him. When I go to sleep at night, I dream of him. How can I get my life back, heavenly Father, when Scott still controls my emotions and rules my heart?"

The thought came to her, Go see him. Settle this once and for all. Yes, it suddenly seemed so simple. She would drive up the coast to Santa Barbara and confront Scott Winslow on his own turf. She would tell him in no uncertain terms how he had hurt her and warn him that he had better straighten his life out if he wanted any peace of mind. Perhaps by putting him in his place, she would save some other unsuspecting woman from suffering the same heartbreak.

But Frannie's bravado was short-lived. When she woke just before dawn the next morning, doubts assailed her. Surely she wouldn't have the strength and courage to face Scott again, let alone give him a piece of her mind. But as she scrambled herself an egg and brewed a pot of coffee, her old resolves returned. She would make the trip, no matter what.

After breakfast she got online and mapped out her trip to Santa Barbara. Amazing these days how she could plot the course from her door to his. She phoned her father and told him she would be dropping Ruggs off for a day or two. When he inquired where she was going, she said simply, "To take care of some old business." Her father didn't ask any more questions, but she knew he suspected what was up.

By 7:00 a.m. she had thrown a valise into the back seat and was on her way. When she dropped Ruggs off at her father's house, Belina came out to the car to collect the dog. "Your dad hinted that you're going to see Scott. Are you sure that's a good idea?"

"I have to," Frannie told her in a matter-of-fact voice. "I can't live like this, wrestling with all these conflicting emotions. Scott has to know he can't treat people this way. Until I tie up these loose ends, I can't get on with my own life."

Belina nodded. "I'll pray for you. See you soon, okay?"

"You bet."

As Frannie wended her way up the coast to Santa Barbara, she seesawed between anger and panic. One minute she was rehearsing what she would say and giving Scott a mental tongue-lashing. The next minute she was asking herself what on earth she was doing, driving up to his Santa Barbara mansion to confront him. "I must be a crazy person, thinking I can accomplish anything by facing him. I'll just make matters worse. What kind of fool am I anyway? Oh, Lord, I'm a lovesick fool, for crying out loud!"

Her hands tightened on the steering wheel until her knuckles gleamed like smooth white stones. "Dear God, I'm doing this because I believe it's the right thing. I'm going with fear and trembling, but I believe You're leading me. If I'm wrong, let me run out of gas or have a flat tire or put a stop sign in my path. Please, don't let me see Scott unless it's Your will!"

It was shortly after noon when Frannie followed the winding driveway up a rugged bluff overlooking the Pacific. Scott's sprawling, Mediterranean-style mansion was reminiscent of a grand villa in Barcelona, with its white stucco exterior, terracotta tile roof, high arched windows and spacious balconies. Colorful gardens accented the manicured lawn. Towering eucalyptus, swaying palms and gnarled oak trees circled the estate. Behind the villa rose the majestic Santa Ynez Mountains.

Frannie's knees felt like jelly as she climbed the steps to the expansive front porch. She breathed another prayer as she knocked soundly on the wide double doors. After a moment, a door opened and a stout, pleasant-faced matron greeted her. The woman's gray-black hair was tied back in a bun and a scalloped apron covered her crisp blue housedress. Her voice was softly lyrical, yet professional. "Yes? May I help you?"

Frannie straightened her shoulders. "I'd like to see Mr. Winslow, please."

"Mr. Winslow?"

"Yes, it's quite urgent."

"Are you here for the wedding?"

"The wedding?"

"If you're a guest, the wedding isn't until this evening. The invitation distinctly said six o'clock."

Frannie felt faint. "You mean, Mr. Winslow is getting married . . . today?"

A frown creased the woman's brow. "You didn't know? You are a friend of the family, aren't you? If not, I really must ask you to —"

"Yes, I'm a friend of Mr. Winslow's," she said quickly. "But we've been out of touch lately. I didn't know about the wedding."

The maid looked relieved. "Oh, I'm glad you're a friend and not some nosy reporter. The family is trying to keep the wedding under wraps, you know. It's just going to be a simple affair with a few close friends and family. They don't want the press getting wind of it and swarming all over the place."

Frannie struggled to keep her voice steady. "Who — who is Mr. Winslow marrying?"

"Why, Miss Vivian LaVelle, of course. That woman is finally going to have the Winslow name. She's done everything in her power for years to become a Winslow, and now she's finally succeeded. Don't you dare tell a soul I said this, but I pity poor Mr. Winslow when he finds out what she's really like."

Frannie reached for the doorjamb and leaned against it for a moment. She refused to pass out on Scott Winslow's porch.

The maid stepped closer, a pinched expression on her face. "Miss, you look ill. You're white as a ghost. Can I get you something? A cup of tea?"

Frannie inhaled deeply. "Yes, that would be good."

The woman led Frannie across the wide marble entry and through a spacious, two-story great hall into a sprawling kitchen. While Frannie sat down at a massive teakwood table, the maid brought her a cup of steaming tea and a slice of buttered toast. "While you drink your tea, I'll go fetch Mr. Winslow for you. He should be back from picking up his tuxedo."

Frannie held up her palm. "No, don't do that. I don't want to disturb him on his wedding day. I'll just drink my tea and be on my way."

The woman shrugged. "Okay, miss, if that's how you want it. I've got lots to do today. The caterers are due anytime now. So I'll check back on you in a few minutes."

It's not how I want it, Frannie reflected darkly, but it's the way things are. It's too late for me to change things now.

As she sipped her tea, she gazed around at the ultra-modern, Spanish-style kitchen with its custom appliances and polished cherrywood cabinetry. As hard as it was to admit, the luxury and opulence of this immense show place reflected the real Scott Winslow. Not the man she knew.

Still, she couldn't help remembering the fun and laughter she and Scott had shared in her bungalow's modest kitchenette. They hadn't needed a wealthy lifestyle or an extravagant residence to be happy. They had enjoyed being together, no matter where they were or what they were doing. At least that's how it had seemed to Frannie. Or maybe she had been so blindly in love, she had missed all the warning signals.

Frannie took another sip of tea, lost in her own reverie, when a familiar masculine voice cut into her thoughts.

"Frannie?"

She whirled around, nearly overturning her cup.

Scott stared down at her, looking as if he had seen a ghost. "Frannie, oh my goodness, it is you! What are you doing here?"

She pushed back her chair and stood shakily, facing him, her face flaming with embarrassment. "I asked your maid not to bother you. I'm not staying, Scott."

He held his arms out, as if to embrace her, but when she backed away, he let his hands fall at his sides. "My maid didn't say a word. I just came in to see if the caterers were here yet."

She took another uneasy step backward, hoping to make her escape before her mortification grew. "For the wedding, you mean."

"You know about the wedding?"

"Yes, your maid told me." Her voice thickened with sarcasm. "Miss LaVelle must be very happy."

Scott grimaced. "She ought to be. She's marrying into a billion dollars."

Frannie grabbed her purse off the table and started for the door. "I'm sorry, Scott. I should never have come. I'm very embarrassed by my bad timing."

He stepped in front of her, his hands raised in a gesture of conciliation. "You can't go. You just got here."

Tears blinded her eyes. "I was a fool to think we still had anything to say to each other. But you kept phoning my house, so I thought maybe —"

"You thought right, Frannie. I've been wanting to talk with you since the night I left the beach house. Why wouldn't you take my calls?"

"How can you ask that? I didn't want to feel humiliated, the way I do right now. A woman does have a little pride, you know. Besides, what was there to say? You lied to me about everything. You deceived me, and I was fool enough to believe you."

"I didn't lie exactly, Frannie. I just omitted some very important details about my life. I had my reasons, and that's what I wanted to tell you on the phone."

"Well, Miss LaVelle told me everything I needed to know, and more. So I don't think there's anything you can add, Scott."

He gripped her shoulders. "Please, Frannie. There's so much more to say. Give me a chance."

Tears coursed down her cheeks. "Nothing you say matters now. You made me fall in love with a man who doesn't exist. I'll never be able to trust my own instincts again."

He ran his palm over her arm, his own eyes glistening. "Frannie, please, I'm sorry I hurt you. I never meant to. I wanted to tell you the truth, but I was afraid it would destroy everything we were building together."

"And it did!"

"Dear Frannie, my wealth has always been a scourge on relationships. I've never known a woman who loved me just for myself. She always saw me through that hideous green filter of my money."

"That's no excuse. I'm not like that."

"I know. I loved the relationship we had. I didn't want to lose it. I thought if I went on pretending I was the man you thought I was, I would eventually become that man. And I did, Frannie. You helped me become the kind of man I always wanted to be."

His closeness taunted her, tantalized her, but she dared not give in to his charm. "You didn't become that man, Scott. You were playing a role. Underneath you were an entirely different man, a man I could never love or respect. Please, let me go!" She pushed against him, but he held her firm.

"I can't let you go until I'm sure you know the whole story."

A sudden weariness overtook her. "Scott, don't tell me any more. I can't bear to hear it. Just let me walk out of your life and forget you ever existed. And you forget about me and go on with your wedding."

He stared quizzically at her. "My wedding?"

"Yes, your wedding to your fiancée, Vivian LaVelle."

He shook his head. "She's not my fiancée."

"Of course she is. She told me so herself."

"She was my fiancée once, but not now."

"I don't understand. She is the bride, isn't she?"

Scott's eyes crinkled with comprehension. "Yes, she's the bride. But I'm not the groom."

Frannie pulled herself free and walked back to the table. She needed to hold on to something for support. "I don't understand. You're talking in riddles. Your maid told me there's going to be a wedding here tonight. She said very definitely that Mr. Winslow is marrying Vivian LaVelle."

"He is." Scott gave her a wry, whimsical smile. "Mr. Winslow *is* marrying Vivian. Mr. *Jason* Winslow is marrying Miss LaVelle."

"Jason?"

"My younger brother. We're a year apart. He and I have sparred back and forth for Vivian's hand for nearly a decade. I'm glad to say that he won the honor, not I."

"You — you're not getting married today?"

"Not unless you want to make it a double ceremony."

"Scott, don't make jokes like that, please. It's too painful."

"Who's joking? I'm dead serious."

She tucked a strand of golden hair behind her ear. "Even if you're not getting married, there's no way I could marry you. You're nothing like the husband I want."

"Are you sure? Will you listen to my story before making such a sweeping judgment?"

She set her purse back on the table. "I suppose. I've come this far."

While she sat down, he went over to the coffeemaker and poured himself a cup of coffee. He brought it over to the table, along with a porcelain teapot. "Frannie, this is going to be a long story. Would you like more tea?"

Chapter Fifteen

"I'm listening, Scott."

He swallowed a mouthful of coffee and set the cup back on the table. In his casual shirt and slacks, with several dark curls straying over his forehead, Scott looked like the carefree beachcomber she remembered. A painful yearning twisted in her heart. If only Scott could say something that would make things right again!

His gaze met hers. "Frannie, I never planned to deceive you. When I moved to the beach, I got caught up in the mystique of being someone else — a carefree drifter, spontaneous and without responsibilities."

"You've told me that already."

"Okay, so I have." He turned the handle of his coffee cup, his thoughts turned inward for several moments. When he spoke again, his voice was husky. "People think being rich is this magical answer to all of life's problems. But in some ways you get caught up in a system where everything is already in place, and you can't change anything. It's bigger than you are, and it takes over your entire existence. For most of my life I accepted the hand fate dealt me, a very lucrative hand, to be sure. I allowed myself to be swept along in the tide of events, because I thought I had no choice.

"But after my mother died I started remembering all the things she had taught me as a child. I recalled the Sunday school class I attended. I knew it wasn't fate I had to reconcile myself to — it was God. I didn't know how to begin that journey back to Him. I just knew I had to separate myself from my life as I had always known it.

"So I broke up with my fiancée, packed a bag and left a note for my family telling them they'd have to manage without me, because I didn't know when I was coming back. I knew we owned some beach houses in Del Mar, so I rented one under another name. It happened to be the one next door to you."

"Until Vivian told me, I never knew I was renting my house from you. But you knew all along."

Scott nodded. "If I had let you know who I was, it would have changed everything between us. My wealth and position would have come between us and kept us apart. I had to see what life could be like without all the baggage. Don't you understand, Frannie? I just wanted us to be two footloose sojourners on the beach getting to know ourselves, each other and God."

"Stop it, Scott." Frannie pushed her teacup away. "All of this idealistic talk is just a subterfuge for your duplicity and deceit. I don't want to hear any more."

He massaged the back of his neck, as if trying to alleviate some deep inner exhaustion. "You win, Frannie. I guess there's nothing I can say to make things right between us again."

"No, Scott, there's not," she replied in a small, pained voice. "Our values are just too different. I admit I don't know a lot about your real estate empire. I've never been one to follow the business reports and newscasts."

"Then how do you know what my moral values are?"

"Your reputation precedes you." She rubbed her knuckles with a nervous agitation. "Even I know about the substandard housing you built and the properties you've allowed to fall into decay and ruin. I know that you have so little compassion for your impoverished tenants that a judge forced you to live in one of your own rat-infested buildings for six months. And, from what I understand, it's still business as usual for the Winslow enterprises. You take advantage of the poor, Scott. You've made your wealth and power by shortchanging the needy and powerless."

Scott's brows knit together, shadowing his eyes. "Those are broad, sweeping judgments, Frannie. Be sure whereof you speak."

"I am sure, Scott. These are things you can't deny." Her words were coming in a rush now; she couldn't hold them back. "And the most unforgivable thing about you is that while your company is fleecing helpless people, you talk so convincingly about the beautiful parks and gardens you want to provide for them. I can't love a double-minded man like that, Scott. All I can feel is pity and disgust —"

Frannie's words broke off. She was on the verge of tears again. She closed her eyes and covered her face with her hands. She hadn't meant to rage on like this, but someone had to put a corrupt man like Scott Winslow in his place. Now maybe she could go home in peace and get on with her life.

"Are you finished, Frannie?" he asked

with unexpected patience.

She picked up her purse and held it tightly in her hands. "Yes, I think I've said quite enough."

He nodded. "I think so, too." He heaved a deep sigh. "As far as I can tell, you've made only one glaring error in your grievous assessment of the Winslow name and empire."

She blinked rapidly. "An error? What was that?"

He pushed back his chair. "I'd rather show you than tell you."

"Show me?"

"Yes. Would you be willing to accompany me to a destination I can't disclose in advance? I promise you'll be safe with me. I'm not a complete ogre."

Her face warmed. "I never said you were."

"But you just painted me as a cruel, despicable man."

"Yes, I suppose I did."

"And yet you feel safe going somewhere alone with me?"

"Yes, but if you keep questioning me, I may change my mind."

Scott went over to an intercom system on the wall and pressed a button. "Dorothy, I'll be going out for a little while. Will you check on the caterers and the flowers? They should be here by now. And you might want to check up on Jason. He should be back by now with our tuxedos."

Scott turned to Frannie. "Ready? Let's go."

Wordlessly she followed him outside and around the villa to a six-car garage where his familiar vintage sports car was parked. "I should have known an out-of-work drifter wouldn't own a rare car like this," she remarked dryly as she slid into the passenger seat.

Neither of them spoke again until they were on Shoreline Drive heading into downtown Santa Barbara. "It's beautiful here," she murmured as they passed gardens, museums, wineries, historic missions and colorful adobes. "I can see why you built your home here."

He nodded. "Yes, it's a little patch of paradise, isn't it?" A hint of cynicism colored his voice. "Hard to believe we have all this beauty and history sandwiched between the mighty ocean and the magnificent mountains. You'd think this would be enough for any man."

"I'm surprised you would want to leave it."

"It wasn't the scenery I was trying to

escape." He turned off the road into a short driveway and parked beside a stucco, mission-style building with a wide courtyard, stone arches and a red-tile roof.

Frannie gazed up at the sign over the massive double doors. "I don't understand, Scott. It says Sea Coast Convalescent Hospital. What are we doing here?"

He helped her out of the vehicle, then took her arm and led her inside. "You want to know the real Scott Winslow, don't you?"

They walked the length of the formal lobby, passing a reception desk where a woman looked up and smiled pleasantly. "Hello, Mr. Winslow. Nice day."

"Hello, Denise," he replied. "Yes, it's a very nice day."

Scott held her arm firmly as he escorted her down a long hallway past elderly and handicapped people on crutches and in wheelchairs. "Hello, mister," one cadaverous woman crooned from her chair. "You come to see me, mister?" She reached out a skeletal hand to Frannie. "How about you, dearie?"

Frannie smiled warmly. "I'm sorry. Maybe another time."

At the end of the hall Scott stopped by a closed door, lowered his head and drew in a deep, shuddering breath.

Frannie could see that he was summoning all of his reserves of mental and emotional strength to open that door. She wanted to ask him who was in there. But she held her tongue.

Finally Scott pushed open the door, took her hand and led her inside. A strong medicinal smell hovered in the air. The room felt too closed, stuffy, the light too scant in spite of the open drapes.

Frannie blinked, her eyes taking in the hospital bed, and beside it, an old man in a wheelchair watching a wide-screen TV. A talk show was playing, the volume turned too low to hear. It was a large, uncluttered room, with two brocade armchairs, a cherrywood dresser and bureau with several bouquets of fresh flowers and a nightstand with a water pitcher, Bible and serving tray with uneaten food.

Scott went over and turned off the television set, then opened the drapes a little wider so that thin sunlight seeped over the stooped figure in the chair.

Frannie stood rooted to the spot, clutching her handbag, her senses alert, anticipating . . . what?

Scott bent over the old man and brushed a kiss on his stubbled cheek. "Hi, Dad. How are you today?"

The grizzled man, dressed in a white cotton gown, velour robe and leather slippers, kept his glazed eyes turned toward the blank television screen. Scott dragged the two armchairs, one at a time, over beside the wheelchair. He nodded for Frannie to take one and he sat down in the other. He leaned forward and took the man's limp hand in his own. "Dad, I want you to meet Frannie. She's a good friend. I know you would like her."

The man didn't move, except to make a clicking sound with his teeth. His gray-white hair erupted from his high, shiny forehead in unruly tufts. Frannie could see now that the old man's mouth was twisted, the left side of his face paralyzed, so that the two sides of his face seemed to have been brought together unevenly.

She could imagine sculpting such a face, her fingers deftly forming his clean, classic features. And then her hand would slip, and the planes and angles of the pliant clay would be displaced just enough to disturb the balance and make the features asymmetric, disturbing. That was what she saw now — a face once strong and remarkable, but something had slipped, shifted, been dislodged, broken.

With his free hand, Scott took Frannie's

slim fingers and squeezed them gently. His voice caught with emotion as he said, "Frannie, I'd like you to meet my father, Scott Winslow Sr."

A shiver of shock traveled down Frannie's spine. As her astonishment cleared, comprehension swept in. This was the man who had given the Winslow empire its ignoble reputation. This was the heartless, oppressive land baron whose name had been desecrated time and again in the press and the media. He had been reduced to *this!*

But he wasn't the Scott Winslow Frannie had fallen in love with!

Frannie touched the man's arm and bent close to his ear. "Hello, Mr. Winslow. I'm pleased to meet you." She looked questioningly at Scott and mouthed the words, "Does he understand what I'm saying?"

"I don't know, Frannie. No one knows. I pretend he does. I have to believe he hears me." Scott leaned in close to his father's contorted face and carefully articulated each word. "I love you, Dad. I wish you could come home with us."

The man sat motionless except for a slight bobbing of his head, his eyes still drifting toward the television set.

Scott's voice rose. "Listen, Dad. Jason is getting married tonight. He's marrying the woman you always wanted me to marry. Vivian LaVelle. He's very happy, and so am I."

Still no response.

"Dad, I want you to know, I've found the woman I want to marry, too. She's sitting right here, Dad." Scott cast a sidelong glance at Frannie and smiled. "I'm hoping someday she'll agree to be my wife."

Her face reddening, Frannie gave him a quick, surprised look. She wanted to comment, to say something, anything, but no words came.

"Dad, would you like me to read to you?" Without waiting for the hint of a response, Scott got up, took the Bible from the nightstand and returned to his chair. He thumbed through the pages, then began reading Psalm 23, his voice resonant with feeling. When he had finished, he closed the book.

Frannie sat unmoving, holding her breath, her hands folded tightly in her lap. Her gaze flitted from father to son and back again. Although the old man's jaw remained slack and his eyes unfocused, Frannie was convinced she saw tears. Tears glazed Scott's eyes, too.

Frannie choked back a sob. She had never felt so deeply moved. She could feel Scott's grieving heart as if it were her own. She had known that pain when she lost her mother. Now, in a different way, Scott had lost his father. How she longed to go to him and take him in her arms and comfort him. But she forced herself to remain silent and still. She sensed that Scott still had more to say to the broken man in the chair.

Scott moved closer to his father's ear, his arm circling the old man's sagging shoulders. "Dad, I don't know if you can hear me or understand me, but I have so much to tell you. Things I never had the courage to say when you were well. I've come to know God in a way I haven't known since childhood. I've gotten acquainted again with the God that Mother loved."

Scott's voice rumbled with emotion. "Listen, Dad. Try to hear me. Jesus loves you. He wants to forgive you for all the wrong things you've done. If somewhere in the depths of your mind you can understand me, please accept God's love and ask Him to forgive you."

Scott took his father's hand in his. "If you understand, Dad, squeeze my hand. Please, Dad."

Frannie met Scott's gaze. His desolate eyes told her there was no response. Scott released his father's hand and stood up, arching his broad shoulders. "We'd better go, Frannie. I've got a wedding to attend."

After saying goodbye to the silent figure in the wheelchair, they left the hospital and headed back to the villa in Scott's vintage automobile. Frannie was still too stunned to absorb all that had just happened. She kept her gaze on the road ahead. Once she murmured, "I never dreamed . . ." But the words eluded her. Finally she remarked, "I wouldn't have expected a man of your father's wealth and position to be in an ordinary hospital like that."

"It's the closest medical facility to our home. I wanted to be able to go see him every day. When he's well enough, I'll bring him home."

Frannie studied Scott's sturdy profile. He was more handsome to her now than he had ever been. "I loved the way you were with your dad. You obviously love him very much."

Scott flashed a wan smile, then turned his gaze back to the road. "I read Scriptures to him every day. Every time I go I tell him Jesus loves him. He would never listen to such talk when he was well. I just pray that he comprehends something I'm telling him now."

"I have faith that he does." Frannie drew

in a deep breath. "I'm sorry I misjudged you, Scott. I still think you were wrong to mislead me about your identity, but I understand better why you did it. And I'm relieved to know you aren't the Scott Winslow who built substandard housing and fleeced the poor."

"Don't be too generous with your praise, Frannie. I'm not guilt-free."

She gave him a guarded look. "What do you mean?"

His knuckles tightened on the steering wheel. "I mean, as his elder son and an executive officer of the company, I should have done more to oppose my father's decisions. I let him and my brother do things their way. They cut corners, overlooked problems and walked a fine line between honesty and fraud. Oh, I protested often enough and threatened to make the truth known. I even said I'd wash my hands of the whole business. But I never put actions to my words."

"But you did, Scott. You finally left. You came to the beach and lived the kind of simple, ordinary life you wanted. That was a means of protest, wasn't it?"

He gave a sardonic chuckle. "Dear Frannie! That was cowardice, plain and simple. Rather than fighting my father and brother, I retreated. Rather than staying and changing the system, I deserted the system. Maybe if I had stayed and fought harder and made things better, my father might not have had his stroke."

Frannie reached over and squeezed his arm. "You can't blame yourself for that, Scott. Your father made his own choices. You had nothing to do with his stroke. Don't take responsibility for something that rests in the hands of God alone."

"I suppose you're right. But I hate feeling so helpless. You don't know what it does to me to see my father — a man who was so strong and powerful — reduced to a feeble invalid." His voice broke on a sob. "Every time I visit him, it tears me apart inside. My brother won't even go see him. Says he wants to remember him the way he was. To me, that's a cop-out."

"It is, Scott. And it's selfish too. I respect you for putting your father's welfare ahead of your own feelings."

"I'm just doing what I have to do. But it's painful to lose someone you love to a slow death."

"I know. My mom had cancer. That was seven years ago. Sometimes I think I still haven't gotten over it. Maybe some things you never get over."

They were both silent for a while. She gazed out at the scenery they had passed before — the wineries and museums and lush landscapes. Everything looked the same. But something within her had changed, and she wasn't sure what it was. It was a bittersweet sensation, as if something had been lost but also gained. Finally she broke the silence with, "Scott, when did your father have his stroke?"

He looked curiously at her. "I thought you knew. It was the day Vivian came to your house looking for me. She brought the news. That's why I left the beach house so quickly. I just threw things in a bag and left with her."

"You left to be with your father? I thought you left to be with her. She never mentioned your father's stroke."

He sighed. "That sounds like Vivian. She deliberately misled you. No wonder you wouldn't take my calls."

"She said she was your fiancée and the two of you were supposed to be married next month."

Scott shook his head. "I broke up with that woman last year before I ever left Santa Barbara." He reached over and took her hand. "Let me get this straight! You thought I was romancing you while I was engaged to someone else?"

Her voice came out light and breathy. "That's how it looked."

"After all that, I'm surprised you came to Santa Barbara to see me."

She twisted her purse strap. "I couldn't get you out of my head, Scott. I thought if I came up here and gave you a piece of my mind, I could go home and get on with my life."

"And now what do you think?"

"I wish I knew." She studied the way the sun etched a golden glow over Scott's rugged profile. Just being with this man stirred a pleasant warmth in her heart. Whenever their eyes met, something tickled inside her. But that didn't mean it was love.

"Things are definitely more complicated than I expected," she admitted. "Nothing's the way it seemed. How can I know how I feel, Scott, when my ideas about you keep changing?"

"I can't answer that, Frannie." His voice was gentle, almost solemn. "But I can tell you how I feel. You heard me tell my father I'm in love with you. And I meant it. The question now is, Where do we go from here?"

Chapter Sixteen

When they arrived back at the villa, the house and grounds were a buzz of activity. The florist was delivering huge bouquets of orchids, carnations and azaleas, along with lush garlands of white roses for the gazebo in the backyard. The caterers were setting out chafing dishes, punch bowls, utensils, silverware, china and crystal on linen-draped tables in the garden. And a technician was adjusting the sound system for the combo that would be performing later.

Scott left Frannie standing alone in the great hall for several minutes while he spoke with Dorothy and the various service people. When he returned, he seemed preoccupied, almost brisk in his demeanor. "They're concerned about whether to have the wedding outside as planned," he told Frannie, "or whether to move everything into the house."

"It's a warm, pleasant day, Scott, and it promises to be a balmy evening, even for October."

"That's what I told them. The white gazebo and exotic gardens are perfect for a wedding. It's where I'd like to be married someday." He gave her a meaningful glance, then rushed on. "So we're going to keep the festivities outside unless a cold front comes in. Or rain. But I don't see a cloud in the sky."

"Neither do I. It should be a wonderful evening for your family, Scott." She turned and took a tentative step toward the foyer.

Scott seized her arm. "Where are you going, Frannie?"

She stopped and looked up at him, her heartbeat accelerating. "It's time for me to go home. If I leave now I may get back to La Jolla before dark."

His grip tightened. "You can't go now. We've just begun to talk. We still have so much to say to each other."

She tried to pull away, but he held her fast.

"Please, Scott, you're going to be busy to-night with the wedding. I'd just be in the way."

"You can't be serious! I want you here. You'll be my guest. Spend the night. We have plenty of rooms. You can have any suite you please. Just say you'll stay."

A thousand arguments collided in Frannie's thoughts. So many pros and cons. There were reasons why she should stay, but even more reasons why she should flee now, before her emotions became more entangled with the cryptic, complex, captivating Scott Winslow.

She looked down at her tailored shirt and stretch jeans. "I don't have a proper outfit for a wedding."

"You didn't bring a change of clothes?"

"Yes, I have some things in the trunk left over from moving . . . a plain black sheath and pumps in the car, but they're not dressy enough for —"

"They'll be perfect. One of my mother's diamond necklaces and earrings will dress it up. You'll be the belle of the ball."

"Scott, I can't!"

"Of course you can. It's settled, Frannie. I've just got you back. I'm not going to let you out of my sight until we've resolved things between us."

The sound of footsteps on the spiral oak staircase distracted them from their conversation. Frannie turned and looked up as a shorter, leaner version of Scott descended the plush stairs in a black tuxedo. The young man's face was narrower than Scott's, but his high cheekbones, straight nose and full lips were unmistakably part of the Winslow heritage. He came striding toward Scott and Frannie with a mischievous smile on his bronze face.

He winked at Scott as he extended his hand to Frannie. "So what have we here, big brother? Is this the mystery woman you've been pining for?"

Scott ignored the innuendo. "Jason, this is Frannie Rowlands. Frannie, my zany brother, Jason. The groom."

They shook hands and exchanged pleasantries for a moment.

"Jason, you don't look half-bad in your tuxedo," Scott observed.

"Thanks, I think. You know how I hate these monkey suits. Good thing I picked up the tuxes myself. When I tried mine on, it needed more alterations. Trousers were too long. I made them do a rush job, or I'd still be there waiting. Hope you have better luck with yours. It's upstairs in your room."

"Guess I'd better go change. The guests will start arriving in another hour."

Jason smiled at Frannie. "You are staying for the nuptials, aren't you, Miss Rowlands?"

"Yes, I guess I am. Scott convinced me. If

you have room for another guest, that is."

Jason held out his hands, palms up. "Look at this place. We could invite half of Santa Barbara if we wished."

"We're only expecting a hundred of our closest friends and colleagues," Scott told her, winking. "We want to keep this simple and private. Not a media event."

Frannie stifled a chuckle. "I've put on a lot of dinner parties, and this is definitely not small or simple."

Scott gently took Frannie's arm. "Let me get Dorothy to show you to your room. And if you give me the keys, I'll get your travel bag from your car. Then you can dress at your leisure and come downstairs when you're ready."

Minutes later, Frannie found herself standing in the midst of a luxurious bedroom with plush white carpeting, a pink canopy bed, floor-length antique mirrors and white French provincial furniture. Off to one side was a sitting room with a balcony overlooking the garden; on the other side was a spacious powder room and bath with a sunken Jacuzzi tub surrounded by tropical fauna.

Frannie kicked off her sandals and did a little pirouette in her bare feet. "I can't believe this! I feel like Cinderella about to go to the ball with Prince Charming!"

She removed her black dress from her travel bag, hung it on the door and examined it closely. "Please don't be too wrinkled. And my pumps . . . I hope they're not scuffed."

After a leisurely bubble bath, Frannie applied her makeup, adding a little extra eyeshadow and mascara. She curled her hair and slipped into her black sheath and pumps. The outfit looked nice enough if she were going to a church social, but hardly fitting for a billionaire's wedding. "How did I get myself into this?" she wondered aloud. "I should just sneak out now, and maybe Scott won't even notice I'm gone."

But moments later, as she descended the spiral staircase, she saw Scott, stunning in his tuxedo, waiting for her, one hand on the oak banister. With a little flourish he held out his hand to her and bowed as if she were a princess. "You look lovely, Frannie. Exquisite. Only one thing is missing."

"What's that?"

"My mother's necklace." He produced a diamond choker from his pocket and fastened it around her neck. Then he handed her two diamond earrings and watched with a smile as she slipped them on.

She tilted her head slightly. "How do I look?"

He beamed. "Like an angel swathed in stars."

She felt color bloom in her cheeks. "No one's ever given me a compliment that was quite so poetic."

"I can't help it. You bring out the poetry in me." He tucked her arm in his. "I think we're ready to join our guests."

Frannie's gaze had been so unswervingly on Scott that she hadn't noticed the wedding guests in all their finery. They were mingling in the foyer and drifting through the great hall toward the stained-glass doors that led to the patio.

"Scott, they're all in formal wear. I can't go out there in this dress."

"Of course you can. You're more beautiful than any woman in the place, including the bride." He led her outside to the gazebo where chairs formed a semicircle around a rose-covered altar. The band was already playing and guests were taking their seats as the setting sun turned the sky a flaming red.

Scott squeezed her arm affectionately. "Frannie, I'm afraid you'll have to survive the ceremony without me. I am the best man, you know. And I'd better give my brother the moral support he needs, considering whom he's marrying. But I'll join you immediately after." He showed her to the first row. "For tonight you'll be family, sitting close to the altar, close to me." His lips curved in a wry smile. "I hope it's a sign of things to come."

She ignored his comment and sat down in the chair he offered. "You go join your brother, Scott. I'll be fine here."

The wedding proceeded without incident. The ceremony was brief, formal and romantic. Even the vain and insufferable Vivian LaVelle looked quite lovely in her designer-original gown. But Frannie hardly heard a word the minister said, for in her imagination, it was she and Scott standing at the altar saying their vows. The fantasy sent her thoughts reeling and her spirits soaring. Oh, if only!

The stars were out and the garden lights twinkling as the reception got in full swing. As the band played an upbeat tempo, Scott escorted Frannie around the garden, introducing her to friends, colleagues and relatives.

But Frannie drew back uneasily when Scott led her over to Jason and his new bride. After Vivian's visit to the beach house, Frannie had no desire for another nasty encounter with the woman. But to her surprise, the bride smiled politely and said, "How nice that you could make it, Miss Rowlands."

"It was a beautiful wedding," Frannie said sincerely.

But while Scott and Jason chatted confidentially, Vivian's smile turned brittle. She leaned close to Frannie and whispered, "You may think you've won, but you'll never have Scott. He's infatuated, but he's no fool. Give him up while you still have your dignity and self-respect."

Frannie rocked back on her heels momentarily, then said through clenched teeth, "I have no designs on Scott. We're friends. That's all." As the men rejoined them, Frannie told Vivian brightly, "I hope you and Jason will be very happy together. You must love him very much."

Vivian turned sharply, picked up her crinolines and flounced away. Jason shrugged and followed after her. Scott drew Frannie into his arms and pulled her close. "What was that all about?"

Frannie averted her gaze. "Nothing important."

"It was something. I saw that look in Vivian's eyes."

"Let's just say your brother's bride isn't too fond of me."

He chuckled. "That's no loss. Say, are you hungry?"

"Famished."

He steered her over to the buffet table. "We'll fill up our plates and see if we can find the most secluded table in the garden."

The long, linen-draped table was brimming with luscious delicacies — beef bourguignonne, glazed ham, Cornish game hens, baked whitefish, shrimp scampi and chicken Parmesan. Candied yams, green bean casserole, rice pilaf, small red potatoes and vegetable lasagna rounded out the menu, along with a variety of salads and breads.

Frannie vowed to try just a little of this and that, but soon her plate was heaped with goodies. She looked helplessly at Scott. "This is a banquet. Too many tempting things I can't resist."

He waved his hand. "Eat all you like. I like a woman who isn't afraid to enjoy her food."

She laughed. "Good thing. Because I may go back for seconds!"

"Don't forget there's all that gooey sweet wedding cake."

"How could I forget? It's as big as a tower and smothered in mounds of icing and little sugar rosebuds. Totally irresistible to someone with a sweet tooth like mine."

"I'm right there with you. Looks like we're both in for a sugar high."

She elbowed him playfully. "At least we don't have to eat and drive."

Scott took both plates and led Frannie to a table at the outskirts of the garden. While Frannie sat down, Scott went to the punch bowl and brought back crystal goblets of sparkling cider. They ate with only the glow of the flickering candlelight between them.

Frannie loved the burnished glow that shimmered over Scott's handsome features. He looked dapper and dashing in his black tuxedo, his chestnut-brown hair swept back, with a single curl straying over his forehead. His dark eyes glinted with merriment as he held up his goblet and toasted her. "To the most beautiful woman under these stars. And to our first wedding together, Frannie. I pray it won't be our last."

As they sipped their drinks, he reached across the table and clasped her free hand firmly in his. "You know, now that I have you here, my dear Frannie, I'm not going to let you go."

She gave him her most guileless smile, baiting him. "You mean you want me to stay here forever?"

"Why not? Every day I'm more convinced we belong together. I'm not just making conversation or handing you a line. I'm speaking from my heart, Frannie."

Her smile faded. "I'm flattered, Scott, but . . ."

"But you're not ready for a commitment, is that it?"

She traced the rim of her goblet. "You must admit we haven't had a typical relationship. Just when I think I know you, something happens and I realize I don't know you at all."

"That's not true. You know me better than anyone. You know the man I want to be. You know me without all the trappings and accoutrements of the Winslow wealth. You know the inner man, the private person I've never revealed to anyone else."

"It's true that I saw a side to you today I loved. The way you were with your father. Your deep compassion for him, even though I know he's disappointed you in so many ways. I love that about you, Scott, that you could reach out to your father at his lowest point, and be there for him."

"I wasn't trying to impress you. I do care deeply for him."

"I know. It was so evident. That's a wonderful trait."

"But it's not good enough, is that it?"

"It's not enough to base a marriage on. Or a future together. Don't you see, Scott? No matter what you say, you're not the man I grew to love during our months on the beach. That man was poor and idealistic, filled with dreams but without the resources to make them come true. But I was convinced he would have done anything in his power to turn them into reality. He would have fought everyone and everything to fulfill his goals. He would have given his very life to make the world a better place for the poor, forgotten people of this land."

"I still feel that way, Frannie. It's my heart's passion."

"Maybe, or maybe not, Scott. You're a man with resources beyond anyone's imagination, but your dreams are just pleasant ideas tucked away for safekeeping. You haven't tried to make them come true. You haven't put everything on the line, you haven't risked all for them, because you're too rooted in your own reality. You say you don't approve of your father's business practices and decisions, and yet you're still part of the company that does things you don't approve of."

Scott released her hand and sat back, a frown creasing his brow. "It's not easy being a man in my position, Frannie. I'm entrenched in this company. It's my life's blood, my past, my future. I'm a vital cog in the machinery that keeps it going, functioning smoothly. Especially now, with my dad incapacitated, I can't just walk away from it and let it flounder. And someday maybe I'll be able to exert the kind of influence that will make a difference."

Frannie fought against a niggling disappointment. She looked away and back again. "See what I mean, Scott? The man I see before me now isn't the impoverished, passionate idealist I knew last summer. The man I see sitting before me now is the rational, pragmatic son of one of America's wealthiest families. How can I relate to you, Scott, when I don't know which man you really are?"

He shrugged. "I guess I'm both men. And, frankly, I don't know how to reconcile the two into the man you want me to be."

"I'm not asking you to change to fit some mold I've created. I want you to be yourself. But don't ask me to commit to you until you know for sure who that man is."

Scott swallowed the last of his drink and pushed back his chair. "This conversation has gotten entirely too solemn for a wedding celebration. Would you like me to show you the rest of the garden under a brilliant ceiling of stars?"

With a titter of laughter, she got up and joined him. Arm in arm they strolled along the narrow footpath through the lush foliage and sheltering oak and eucalyptus. The band was playing romantic ballads in the distance, the music blending with the muffled voices of the wedding guests. The melodies wafted on the same crisp sea breeze that rustled Frannie's hair and brought out goose bumps on her bare arms. Or was it Scott's closeness that electrified her senses?

After a while, he stopped and pointed to the sky. "Do you see the Big Dipper up there?"

"And there's the North Star. They're so clear tonight."

His arm encircled her waist. "I ordered them just for you."

She gazed up at him, studying the way the shadows and moonlight played on his face. "You didn't have to do that for me, Scott. I only needed a star or two, not a whole sky."

He pulled her against him, so close that she could feel his heart beating against her breast. "I'd give you the galaxies if I thought it would make you happy, Frannie."

Her lips parted to offer a response. But before she could make a sound, his lips came down on hers, soft, gentle, moving over her mouth with exquisite tenderness. In that blissful moment, she yearned for nothing more than to melt in his arms, as pliant as the supple clay she molded with her fingers.

"I love you, Frannie," he whispered against her ear. "I need you more than life itself. Tell me you love me, too."

Dazzled, delighted, she struggled to catch her breath. "I do, Scott. I love you with all my heart."

"That's all I wanted to hear, my darling." He kissed her earlobes, her eyes, her hair, then moved back again to her lips. She relaxed, returning the kiss, luxuriating in the taste of his lips, the encompassing warmth of his embrace.

This was where she belonged, where she yearned to remain forever . . . with this man she cherished and adored. Even with her eyes closed, she saw the spangling stars, flaming and bright, exploding like fireworks. They were more brilliant in her heart than they had ever been in the heavens.

It occurred to Frannie that maybe it was time to listen to the yearnings of her heart rather than to the cold voice of reason. Maybe Scott Winslow was the man for her after all.

Chapter Seventeen

Frannie lost track of time in Scott's arms. Had they been lost in their embrace for mere moments, or hours, or forever? At last she pulled away, her senses still reeling, her legs unsteady.

Scott kept his arms loosely around her waist. "Are you okay?"

"Yes." She rubbed her forehead. "Just a little dizzy."

"It can't be the sparkling cider." He smoothed her hair back from her forehead. "Maybe it's the intoxication of love."

She smiled. "That must be it."

"We'll go back and sit down." He kept his arm around her as they walked back to their table. "Would you like something more to drink?"

"No. Actually, I think I'll use the powder room."

"It's right off the great hall, to the right.

Would you like me to show you the way?"

"No, I'll find it."

Wending her way through the milling guests, Frannie returned to the villa and found the powder room. To her amazement, it looked like a fancy sitting room, with velvet wallpaper on three walls and a floor-to-ceiling mirror on the fourth. She uttered a little exclamation of admiration as she gazed around at the posh furnishings — an overstuffed sofa and love seat, polished end tables and ruffled lamps. "This gives new meaning to the term, 'reading room,' " Frannie remarked to another guest, who was on her way out.

The stout, middle-aged woman checked her hem in the mirror and smiled. "If you're looking for the bathroom, this is it. Just keep going around the corner."

"Thanks. I was afraid I had stumbled into the wrong place. The maid's quarters, or something."

"This house is like that. Incredible. They could turn it into a hotel and still have room to spare." The woman patted a curl into place, then headed for the door. She paused and looked back at Frannie. "That's what you get when you're filthy rich. Makes the rest of us look like paupers, even with our million-dollar estates."

Frannie held back a chuckle. What would the woman think if she knew Frannie's "luxury mansion" was a modest rented beach house with a tiny bathroom, sagging porch and clogged chimney?

Moments later, Frannie was washing her hands when she heard two women enter the powder room. She couldn't see them, but they were talking loudly and sounded as if they had been celebrating a little too heavily.

Frannie was about to leave when she heard one woman call the other, *Vivian.* Frannie's breath caught. Not Vivian LaVelle! She was the last woman Frannie wanted to face again. Stepping back into the shadows, Frannie waited, hoping she could slip out unnoticed after the two women left. But they showed no signs of hurrying, so Frannie gritted her teeth and listened.

"Oh, Vivian," one woman exclaimed, her voice slurring, "why did they put a mirror like this in here? What woman wants to see this much of herself?"

"Miranda, you look gorgeous. You just want somebody to tell you so."

Yes, Frannie acknowledged silently, withdrawing farther into the shadows, the second voice was definitely Vivian's.

"Of course, darling. And you look absolutely ravishing in that wedding gown. I bet it set Jason back a pretty penny."

"He wanted me to have the best. Who was I to argue?"

"That husband of yours is a gem. Always extravagant. And generous to a fault. He's a treasure. Hold on to him."

"I intend to."

There was silence for a moment. Frannie wondered if they were leaving. Then the first woman spoke again.

"I'd better sit down here a minute, Vivian. That champagne! You know me. I couldn't get enough of the bubbly. You tell Jason I'll come to his wedding every day if he puts on a spread like this."

"I think you had a little too much, Miranda."

"Way too much. Sit here with me for a minute, Vivian."

"Just for a minute. I have other guests, you know." A pause, then: "Speaking of guests, Miranda, did you see that woman with Scott Winslow?"

"A pretty thing. Who is she? I haven't seen her before."

"She's nobody you'd know . . . nobody you'd wish to know. She's a charlatan if I ever saw one. A real gold digger. Did you see those diamonds she was wearing? I happen to know those belonged to Scott's mother."

"You can't be serious."

"I'm dead serious. I'd seen the old woman wear them a hundred times."

"My goodness, Vivian, how did she get her hands on them?"

"I don't know. But she's got Scott duped — you can be sure of that."

"I'm shocked. The woman has no shame, flaunting the Winslow jewels like that. And at a Winslow wedding! Can you imagine such audacity?"

"Mark my words, Miranda. That shallow twit doesn't have the slightest idea what it means to be a Winslow."

"I'm sure she doesn't, Vivian."

"You can tell she has no class or breeding. If she marries into this family, she'll be swallowed up. Her life won't be her own. The Winslows will devour her and spit her out."

"Like an eggshell in an omelet. That's what my mother used to say, Vivian. You know how distasteful finding an eggshell can be."

"I'm going to keep my eye on that woman, Miranda. I swear I will. I haven't given up ten years of my life to let some other woman get her hands on the Winslow money. Miranda, are you ready to go yet?

Jason will be looking for me."

"Yes, Vivian, I'm feeling better. Who knows? Maybe I'll have another glass of champagne."

"Miranda, you take the cake." She gave an icy little twitter. "Speaking of cake, it's time to cut mine. Come. It'll go well with your champagne."

"Oh, heavens, yes. Cake and champagne. Delightful!"

After the two women had gone, Frannie remained for several moments in the shadowed corner of the powder room before stirring. Her body felt as paralyzed as her mind. The women's conversation echoed inside her like a death knell. How could they have been so vicious? What had she done to elicit such cruelty? Worse than their arrogance was the frightening possibility that they could be right. To involve herself with a Winslow man could spell heartache and calamity for her just as it had for Scott's mother.

Frannie gazed at her reflection in the mirror. Her face looked blanched, her lips tight, her eyes wide with alarm. Her stricken expression reminded her of a deer caught in the blinding glare of headlights just before it's struck. The analogy was all too real, the bitter truth staring Frannie in the face. Entertaining the idea of a life and future with the wealthy, powerful Scott Winslow was like walking into the path of an oncoming truck. There was no way she could survive intact. At least not as the person she was now. To fit in with these affluent people and become part of this lavish lifestyle, she would have to become a different person, someone she wasn't sure she could respect, someone like Vivian.

With her spirits ebbing, Frannie returned to the garden, but she no longer felt like partaking of the festivities. If only she could leave right now and drive home. But the hour was late, and it had already been a long day. She looked among the throng for Scott and spotted him zigzagging through the crowd balancing two plates of wedding cake.

"Here you are!" he said as he handed her a plate. "I thought maybe you had gotten lost. I hope my directions weren't that misleading."

"No, they were fine. I'm sorry. I lost track of time."

"No problem." His eyes crinkled with warmth. "I missed you. I'll get us some punch and we can go back to our table."

"No, Scott. I'm really not hungry for cake. I was thinking of . . . of going to my room and making an early night of it."

He looked dumbfounded. "Aren't you feeling well?"

She touched her forehead. "I do have a headache. I hope you don't mind, Scott."

He set their cake on the table, then slipped his arm around her shoulder and drew her close, his chin nuzzling her hair. "I was counting on spending a few more hours together in this romantic setting, but I do understand."

"Thanks, Scott. I'm sure I'll be fine in the morning."

"I hope so. We still have a lot to talk about. And plans to make, now that we know how we feel about each other."

"Plans?"

"For our future. I want us to make a life together, Frannie. Surely you want that, too."

Her muscles tensed. "I can't think about it tonight, Scott. Too much has happened. I can't take it all in."

He turned to face her and took her hands in his. "Would you like me to walk you up to your room?"

"No, I can find it. Oh, and one more thing." She unfastened the diamond necklace, removed the earrings and placed them in Scott's hand. "These belong to you."

"You don't have to take them off now. You can leave them in your room, if you like."

"No, Scott. I don't want to pretend to be someone I'm not."

His brows furrowed. "You didn't enjoy wearing them? They looked stunning on you."

She struggled to keep her lower lip from quivering. "I guess I'm just one of those plain-Jane girls. What you see is what you get. I don't need million-dollar diamonds, Scott. I'm happy in rhinestones and dime store jewelry."

Bewilderment shadowed his handsome features. "That doesn't mean you can't get used to the real thing."

"That depends on what the real thing is, Scott. For me, the real thing is what we had together on the beach when we were counting our pennies, trusting the Lord and surviving on a pittance. We were thriving then, Scott, having the time of our lives. That was real to me. But now I realize that this is your real world and that was just pretend. I'm not sure this could ever be my world, Scott."

"It can be. Just give us a chance, Frannie." He wrapped her in his arms and kissed her cheek.

She broke away, blushing as she noticed other guests glancing their way. "We have to pray about it, Scott," she said in a small, hushed voice. "We need to put our future in God's hands."

"I agree. I promise you, I'll be doing a lot of praying tonight."

"Me, too." She pivoted before he could notice the tears in her eyes. "Good night, Scott."

As he caught her hand for a lingering moment, she realized he had never looked more handsome and debonair. "Sleep well, my darling." His gentle, resonant voice wrapped itself around her heart. "I love you, Frannie. I'll see you in the morning."

With blinding tears, she slipped awkwardly through the press of laughing, partying guests, and made her way up the grand spiral staircase to her room.

After locking the door, she undressed and slipped into her cotton nightgown, suddenly too tired even to wash off her makeup. She climbed into bed, pulled the downy comforter over her and tried to sleep. But as exhausted as she felt, sleep eluded her. She could hear the band playing in the garden, the sweet, sentimental ballads accented by garbled voices and laughter. It was as if the world were going on without her, and she had no idea where she belonged in that opulent, paradoxical sphere. Or whether she even belonged at all.

Finally, growing restless, she got up and walked over to the sliding glass door and looked out. The sky was still ablaze with stars. Quietly she opened the door and stole out onto the balcony. It was amazing. Like a tiny bird perched on a limb, she could look down on the entire wedding celebration, and no one could see her watching.

For a long while, she observed the festivities below in curious fascination — dozens of guests milling about, chatting, dancing, laughing, eating and drinking. It was as if God were giving her a glimpse of a world she had never inhabited. She spotted Scott in the crowd, moving from table to table, conversing with guests, smiling, chuckling, as if he had forgotten she had even been there.

Her curiosity gave way to a sense of loneliness and isolation. What was she doing in this place? She surely didn't belong here. But if not here, then where? The question of where she belonged plagued her these days.

Frannie stepped back inside her room and curled up in a velvet love seat beside the open sliding door, where she could still feel a refreshing breeze. It was time to take her eyes off people and circumstances and focus them on her heavenly Father.

"Lord, I really need to talk with You," she said aloud, her tenuous voice jarring the stillness. "You know how confused I've been since Daddy remarried. I don't know where I belong anymore. I can't go back home and be Daddy's little girl, taking care of him the way I did after Mother died. He has Juliana now. And Belina. A whole new family. He doesn't need me anymore.

"But I can't stay here with Scott in his palatial villa, surrounded by his snobbish friends and all the trappings of wealth. I know now I don't belong in his world, either. I could never be a jaded, society-minded rich girl.

"But who am I then, Lord? I don't know anymore. Maybe all I want to be is the girl on the beach, with just the sun and sea and my sculptures around me, and no one to answer to but You, Father. Is that what You want for me? Help me to know what to do."

When she had finished praying, Frannie climbed back into bed and slept soundly until the first rays of dawn washed over her. She got up and looked out the sliding door at the red streaks breaking through the azure heavens. The world was a silent place this morning, devoid of humanity. God alone was evident in the vivid splendor of His sunrise. Apparently no one else in the house was up yet.

A thought occurred to Frannie. If I leave now, I won't have to face Scott and all his questions. I won't have to give him an answer about committing to a relationship, or see the disappointment in his eyes when I tell him I have no idea what God wants for us.

Frannie dressed quickly and threw her things into her travel bag. She found a sheet of stationery in the dresser and, with a trembling hand, scribbled a note to Scott.

"I'm sorry. This was a mistake. It's over, Scott. Please don't call me or contact me. Don't make it any harder for us than it is. Frannie."

Gingerly she stole downstairs. The house was silent, no one in sight. She slipped out to her car, tossed her things in the trunk and minutes later was on the freeway, heading south to San Diego.

As she drove, she vowed that she would forget Scott. She would throw herself into her work — her sculpting and her classes at the university. She would spend more time in church, and with her father and sisters, and Belina. And she would learn to accept Juliana as part of her family. She would carve out a productive, worthwhile life for herself and have no one to answer to but God.

Whatever it took, she would put Scott Winslow out of her mind forever. But, even as she made her resolves, she knew that getting him out of her heart would be infinitely more difficult.

Chapter Eighteen

Last night I dreamed my mother was still alive. We were sitting in the garden talking together, and I kept marveling at how wonderful it was to see her and be able to tell her all the things I felt about her, and how much I loved her. I touched her skin and looked into her eyes, and told her how strange it was that I had somehow believed she was dead; I had dreamed her death, and now I knew it wasn't so. She was still here with me; we still had time together for all the things I yearned to do with her.

And then suddenly I awoke, and she was gone. I realized with an ache in my heart that the reality was reversed. My mother was dead, buried over seven years now, and alive only in my dreams.

Frannie set down her journal and let the pen fall from her fingers. She hadn't written in this thumb-worn book in months, maybe even years. She had packed it and brought it with her to the beach house, then stuck it in a drawer and forgot about it. Now that she had come across it again, she felt compelled to write and express the inexpressible in her heart.

Why was it, in the two months since she had fled Scott's Santa Barbara villa, she grieved her mother's death as much as she mourned losing Scott? Hadn't she already anguished over her mother for seven long years? Why were the memories assailing her afresh — the haunting images of that slow, dreadful dying and her own helplessness as she watched the cancer ravage her mother's body? There had been nothing she could do but stand by and watch. God help her, she lost her mother bit by precious bit and couldn't change a thing. How she hated being powerless. To this day the idea plagued her that there must have been something she could have done.

But now she couldn't stop wondering why the one loss had become entangled with the other, so that she wasn't sure which one she mourned the most.

She hadn't lost Scott, of course. She had deliberately set him free, and herself free, as well. After all, they came from two vastly different worlds. To try to blend their lives would only have brought heartache and pain. And she had had enough pain for two lifetimes.

Scott had phoned the day after his brother's wedding, but she had told him she didn't want to see him. It had to end here and now, because she couldn't imagine the two of them becoming husband and wife. Better not to draw things out, she told him, because the misery would only be worse.

His reply still tolled in her mind. "You're making the biggest mistake of your life, Frannie, and someday, when it's too late, you're going to realize it."

Since then, every morning when she awoke, she silently told herself, Letting Scott go wasn't a mistake. I did the only thing I could do. It's for the best. She had to believe it. The alternative was unthinkable.

On most days she refused to let her mind dwell on Scott and what might have been. She kept herself busy with her art classes and a new commission for the La Jolla library. But now, with Christmas in the air, she was feeling a tad sentimental. She would probably leave the beach house and move back home for a week or two, to enjoy the holidays with her family. Her father always insisted on a live, ten-foot tree, decorated to the max, with loads of presents piled high around it.

Besides, the beach house was drafty these days, as the seasonal winds and rains assailed it. It had become a lonely place, especially without Scott in the neighboring bungalow.

So, on a Tuesday morning, one week before Christmas, Frannie phoned her father and said, "Daddy, how would you like a house guest over the holidays? Two, in fact, if you count Ruggs."

As she expected, her father was overjoyed at the prospect of having his little girl home again. And Frannie had to admit, she was looking forward to it as much as he.

"Well, Ruggs, Daddy wants us home for Christmas." Frannie tossed her empty suitcase on the bed and opened it. Item by item, she folded her garments and laid them in the case. Shirts, jeans, dresses, sweaters, nightwear, lingerie. Just enough for a two-week stay.

Just as she was deliberating whether she would need a second travel bag, there was a loud knock on her door. She brushed back her tangled hair and looked down at Ruggs. "Looks like we have company, boy. What do you wanna bet it's someone selling something?"

Ruggs barked, made a little circle, then bounded out of the bedroom, yipping eagerly. Frannie followed him to the door and grabbed his collar. "Quiet, Ruggsy. You'll wake the dead!"

She opened the door and stared up into the face of Scott Winslow. He stood on the porch in a navy business suit and tan overcoat, looking as if he had stepped out of a sophisticated men's fashion magazine.

"Scott!" Frannie gazed down at her own rumpled flannel shirt and clay-streaked sweatpants. She tucked a flyaway strand of gold hair behind her ear. "What are you doing here?"

"I'm a man on a mission, Frannie. May I come in?"

She backed awkwardly into the room and swept out her hand. "Of course. Come in. It's cold out there."

He strode immediately over to the fireplace and held out his hands before the crackling flames. "I see your chimney is working well these days."

She smiled wryly. "Someone once gave me good advice about keeping the flue clear." She approached him. "May I take your coat?"

He shrugged off his overcoat and handed it to her. She hung it on a hook by the door.

"Please sit down. May I get you something to drink? Coffee? Hot cocoa?"

He settled on the couch. "No, thanks, Frannie. I'd just like a little conversation."

She sat down on the overstuffed chair. "If I'd known you were dropping by, I would have . . . Well, I wouldn't be looking like this."

He grinned. "You look great. Fresh and natural and very attractive."

Her face warmed. "I was just packing. . . ."

"You're leaving the beach house?"

"Just over Christmas. Going home to my dad's for the holidays."

"That's good. It's exactly what a daughter should do. How is your father?"

"Fine. Healthy. Happy with his new wife." She paused, her forehead creasing. "How is your father?"

Scott gazed down at his hands. "He died a week after you saw him."

"I'm so sorry," she said compassionately.

"I hope something I said about accepting Christ's love got through to him."

"We have to trust that it did."

"I'm trying. It's hard. My father and I were never close, but I grew up thinking of him as invincible and indestructible. He was the captain of our ship, so to speak, our inveterate taskmaster and a crafty old curmudgeon. He ruled with an iron hand, and I never found the courage to cross him. But I miss him more than I ever thought possible."

Instinctively Frannie leaned over and squeezed Scott's hand. "I know. After all these years, I still miss my mother."

"I know you do. I guess it's just going to take time for both of us."

"They say time is the great healer, but I'm not so sure."

"Neither am I. But I do believe God is."

Frannie nodded. "Yes. He walks us through the darkness, holds our hand through the shadow of death."

Scott sat forward and folded his hands in a businesslike fashion. "I didn't come to talk about my dad, Frannie." He cleared his throat and assumed a professional tone. "I have a proposition for you."

Frannie winced inwardly. She wasn't up for any verbal sparring over their relationship. She had struggled too hard these past two months to distance herself emotionally from him. "Please, Scott, don't dredge up the past."

"That's not what this is about, Frannie. I have a business proposition for you."

"Business?"

"Yes. I'd like to commission you to do a sculpture of children at play. It could be three children, five, whatever you choose. We would like sketches of your design by the end of January, if possible. And if our committee likes what they see, we'll offer you a hefty sum that I hope you won't be able to resist."

Frannie's mind whirled with questions. "I don't understand, Scott. What do you want this sculpture for?"

He gave her a cryptic smile. "It's a long story, Frannie. My brother and I inherited our father's company. To my surprise, my father gave me controlling interest. I let my brother know there would be sweeping changes. I would no longer support my father's shady practices or heartless tactics. I appointed a new board of directors and new executive officers, men of honor and integrity. From now on, Winslow Enterprises will be a company I can be proud of."

"That's wonderful, Scott. It sounds like you have your work cut out for you."

"Well, I've put good men in charge so that I can focus my attention on a personal project that's dear to my heart."

"What's that?"

"Remember my sketchbook of drawings? The community I wanted to create for people who can't afford housing in today's overpriced market?"

"Of course, I remember. You wanted to build parks and playgrounds and make a beautiful place for poor families and children to live."

"And that's what I'm going to do, Frannie. I'm going to build a planned community with quality homes, apartments, parks and walking areas, plus neighborhood shops and businesses that will offer local job opportunities."

"What a wonderful idea, Scott. Where will you build?"

"Actually, it's not terribly far from here. Maybe a two-hour drive."

"Then you'll be commuting from Santa Barbara?"

"No, I'm hoping to move to this area."

"Well, then tell me! Where is it?"

"I've purchased a large piece of property in the desert, near Yucca Valley. It's a prime area for future home developments. It offers gorgeous scenery and wide open spaces, but it's a close commute to nearby cities. The houses will cost half as much in the desert as they do in Los Angeles. And we'll offer low-interest loans and special endowments to needy-but-deserving families. It'll be a prototype of the kind of housing developments

I want our company to build from now on."

"That's fantastic, Scott. I'm so proud of you. And you want this sculpture of children for your planned community?"

"Exactly."

"I'm finishing a commission now, but I should be able to have preliminary drawings to you by the end of January."

"Great. That's what I wanted to hear." Scott shifted, as if mentally switching his concentration to something else. He looked at her, his gaze frank, unnerving. "Listen, Frannie, there's something else."

Oh, no, here it comes! She steeled herself.

"I just wanted to tell you that you were right about me."

"Right about . . . what?"

"You told me once that it was time to follow my passions and stop living in the shadow of my father and brother. It was time for me to find the work and life that God had planned for me."

"I don't remember saying that exactly."

"But that was the message I got. And since my father's death, I've done that, Frannie. For the first time in my life I'm excited. I'm eager. I have a driving desire for the work God wants me to do."

"I'm glad for you, Scott."

"The motivation started with you,

Frannie. In a sense, you've given me back my life. You've made my life richer, because I've tapped into a passion and joy for the work I was created to do."

"Scott, I think you're giving me way too much credit."

He stood and walked over to the window and looked out. "I love being back in this cottage, Frannie. It reminds me of our days here on the beach last summer. Those were the best days of my life."

"They were good days, but like everything, they came to an end."

He strode back over to her, seized her hands and pulled her to her feet. He fingered her tousled hair and touched her cheek with his fingertips. "I've missed you, Frannie."

She turned her face away. "No, Scott, please. Let's keep our visit casual, uninvolved."

"I can't do that, Frannie. I tried coming in here and acting businesslike. I tried pretending we're only friends. But it's not working."

"That's all we can be, Scott. That's why I left the villa without saying goodbye. I knew you would try to persuade me . . ."

"Don't you see, Frannie? All the good things . . . I want to share them with you —

every exciting adventure, every joy and surprise, every rare and wonderful experience that God has planned for us."

"Please, stop it, Scott. Don't include me in your plans."

"But I must, Frannie. I can't imagine my life without you." He clasped her face in his hands. "Look at me, Frannie. Tell me you don't feel the love. It's like static electricity. It makes the air between us sizzle."

"Scott, don't —"

"I haven't finished telling you my plans. I've purchased a beach house near here. Actually, my company already owned it, and now I'm buying it for myself. For us. It's bigger than this one. A bungalow for two. You and me, Frannie. You see, I want to live the simple life just as you do."

"That's just a dream, Scott."

"No, not anymore. I have people in place in my company to execute my plans, so I can be with you in our beach house. While you sculpt fine works of art, I'll plan and design breathtaking communities. Together we'll make life more beautiful for so many people. But I want to start with us. I want to marry you and give you and our children a beautiful life. Please say you'll at least think about it . . . and pray about it."

Tears welled in Frannie's eyes. "Scott, I

told you it wouldn't work between us. Why won't you believe me?"

"Because I don't think you believe it yourself, my darling." He removed his handkerchief and gently blotted the tears in her eye. "I think you're responding out of fear, not conviction."

"How can you say that? You don't really know me."

"I think I do, Frannie. Tell me if I'm wrong. You've always had to be in control. After your mother died, you took care of your father. You ran the household, planned and fixed the meals. You had to be in charge of your environment and of all the people in your life."

"That's not fair, Scott. You make me sound obsessive —"

"When your father remarried, you moved out of the house because it meant you would no longer be in charge, no longer running the show. So you moved to this isolated beach house where you could be in charge again, and not have to answer to anyone else."

"It wasn't like that."

"You told me once that you wouldn't marry me because you couldn't accept my lifestyle. But aren't you really afraid it would mean subjecting yourself to a world you can't control?"

"That's ridiculous."

"Is it? I think you're afraid to step into an uncertain, unpredictable world. You're afraid of being hurt again, the way you were hurt when you couldn't control the circumstances of your mother's death."

Frannie was weeping now. "How dare you compare my mother's death to this!"

Scott led her over to the couch, and they both sat down. He handed her his handkerchief, then slipped his arm around her and drew her against his chest. "I'm not trying to open old wounds, sweetheart, but I've been thinking about this for a long time, and the pieces are beginning to fall into place. You lost the person most precious to you. Since then, if you can't control every detail of your circumstances, you run."

"I do not!"

He tilted her tearstained face up to his and lightly kissed her lips. "My darling girl, it's as if you're holding a bird tightly in your hand because you're afraid of losing it. What you're really doing is smothering it, killing it. You need to open your hand and let it fly where it will. Being fully alive means taking risks, Frannie. Loving someone means risking being hurt, risking losing them someday. But to never take the risk is to deny yourself the happiness God wants you to have."

He took her hands and opened her fingers, one by one. "You need to open your hands and receive what God has for you. He's offering you a wonderful, unpredictable life and a man who loves you with all his heart. I confess that the man's not perfect. He's made mistakes and will make mistakes in the future. But he's a man who loves you and loves God and wants to make his life count for something."

"Scott, you're making this so hard. I just don't know — !"

"It's not hard. Open your hands, Frannie. Open your heart. Let God show you the way. Relax in Him. Accept what He brings you, with open arms. Accept me, Frannie. Let me be part of your life. Let me take care of you the way you've always taken care of others. Let me love you with all the love I have to give."

She wiped the tears from her eyes. "I do love you, Scott, but I can't let down my guard and agree to something I may regret later. I'm sorry. I have to be sure."

With a heavy sigh, he stood and gazed down at her. "I'm sorry, too. I can offer no guarantees, Frannie. Except this. You can't enjoy life until you release yourself to it, just as you can't trust God until you surrender yourself to Him. It's a lesson I'm still learning. Happiness and fulfillment come when you give yourself unreservedly to God, to the person you love and to life itself."

He crossed the room and collected his coat, then pulled it on and walked to the door. Ruggs bounded over to him and barked. Scott bent down and scratched the dog's ears. "Do me a favor, Ruggsy. Take good care of your master, okay? That's a good boy."

Scott looked back at Frannie with tenderness and yearning. "I'm going over to my bungalow for an hour or two to clear out my things. Then I'll be driving back up to Santa Barbara. If you change your mind, you know where I'll be."

She got up and walked to the door. She felt as if she were moving in a dream. She didn't want him to go, but she couldn't ask him to stay. Impulsively she kissed him on the cheek. He pulled her to him and kissed her hard on the mouth, then released her. He pushed open the door and stepped out onto the porch. "Goodbye, Frannie. You'll always be in my prayers."

"And you'll be in mine." She covered her mouth as he turned and descended the steps. She watched until his car pulled out of the narrow driveway and disappeared down the road.

After Scott had gone, Frannie slipped on her windbreaker and went outside, Ruggs following at her heels. She couldn't stand the confines of her cabin. She had to get some fresh air to clear her head.

She walked down to the beach and gazed out at the cold, muted blue ocean, the spumy tide rushing in, covering the sand, then retreating, to start the process all over again. Back and forth, an endless pattern, the rhythm of life. It was the way she felt. She kept going back and forth, stepping out in faith, then drawing back in fear. Where was she going, and would she ever have the courage to reach her destination? She gazed up at the huge dome of sky, cloudy and gray, stretching from horizon to horizon, a vast, unremitting gray. Like the sky, her life felt shrouded in gray, murky shadows. When would the sun come out? When would she see things clearly?

She folded her arms to stave off the biting wind, but still she shivered with a deep, bone-chilling cold. As she watched the slow, graceful dance of the waves, she imagined herself lying on a surging swell, floating, letting the tide take her where it would. Trusting God was like that. Relaxing on His promises, His truth, His Word. The apostle Peter was afraid, but he stepped out by faith and walked on water to Jesus. Could she do that? Step out in spite of her fears?

She remembered Jesus' words, "I will never leave you, nor forsake you. . . . My peace I give to you; not as the world gives. . . . Let not your heart be troubled, neither let it be afraid."

Looking up at the ashen sky, she whispered, "Dear God, what do You want me to do? I love Scott, and I don't want to lose him, but I am so afraid. . . ." Even as she said the word, the fragment of another Scripture came to her. "Perfect love casts out fear." The truth hit hard. She would never be able to love fully until she released her fear.

The thought came to her. What do you really want, Frannie? If Scott is the man you love, don't run away. Run to him. As fast as you can.

She walked back to her cottage, but she couldn't bring herself to go inside. Instead, she stooped down and gave Ruggs a hug around the neck. "What do you think, boy? Do you want Scott to be your master?"

The shaggy dog barked loudly.

She smiled grimly. "I should have known better than to ask you." She straightened her shoulders, sucked in a breath and lifted her chin. "Okay, Ruggsy, maybe it's time I stepped out and walked on water. Come on, boy!"

As she hiked down the beach toward Scott's bungalow, she became aware of a growing excitement, a sense of anticipation filling her heart, replacing the fear. She was shivering with cold when she finally knocked on Scott's door.

He answered with a smile of surprise. "Frannie!"

She kept her arms folded across her chest, but couldn't stop trembling. Flustered, she blurted, "I, um, have this chimney that's clogged. And the smoke . . . the smoke is coming into my house. And it's really not a safe place to stay . . . you know, with all that smoke billowing in. And I know you're an expert with blocked chimneys. So I was wondering if you'd like to help a damsel in distress."

His grin widened. "I'd be more than happy, if that damsel is you."

Her teeth chattered. "W-well, maybe I c-could just come inside while the smoke clears."

He stepped aside. "I think we can arrange that."

She drew back. "I don't want to trouble you. I know you're packing."

"No trouble at all. I can pack anytime."

"Well, maybe you wouldn't have to pack at all."

"Really? Maybe you'd better come in and we'll discuss it." He took her arm and led her inside. Ruggs scurried in after her.

"What a nice, roaring fire." She walked over and put her palms up to the flames. "Ah, that feels good."

He came up behind her and helped her off with her jacket. "You won't need this. It's very warm in here."

She nodded. "Yes, very warm."

He turned her around to face him, then ran his hands up and down her arms. "You are cold."

She gazed up at him, searching his eyes. "I walked on water to get here."

"Did you now? That took an amazing amount of faith."

"Did it? I just relaxed, opened my hands wide and stepped out . . . and here I am."

He smiled, his eyes glistening. "I'm very proud of you, Frannie." He smoothed back her hair, tipped her chin up to his and kissed her tenderly. "Do you have any idea how much I love you?"

"As much as I love you?"

"Maybe we should sit down and discuss it." He led her over to the sofa and they sat down. Ruggs came bouncing over and laid his head on Scott's lap.

"He's part of the package. You know the old saying, 'Love me, love my dog.' "

Scott massaged Ruggs's head. "I think I can manage that. How about it, Ruggsy? Do you approve of me marrying your master?"

Ruggs lifted his head and gave a long, ear-splitting howl.

Frannie and Scott both laughed.

He drew her close and murmured against her ear, "I'll take that as a yes."

Epilogue

December Twenty-five

Dear Family and Friends,

I'm usually too busy writing sermons to write Christmas letters. But so much has happened in the Rowlands family this year that I figured I'd better send a letter to catch you up on the latest news.

It's been an exciting and eventful year for the Rowlands clan. In June, Cassandra and Antonio had their first child, a boy, little Daniel Pagliarulo, a fine, handsome lad with his father's dark hair and his mother's blue eyes. It's quite an experience being a grandfather.

I became a grandfather again in July when Brianna married attorney Eric Wingate and the two of them adopted his little niece, Charity. What a joy that precious child is — only three years old and yet she carries the wisdom of the ages in her eyes. And she's a mischievous little bundle to boot, playing hide-and-seek with her grandpa and looking for candy bars in my shirt pocket — naturally, I always keep a stash of goodies for when she comes to visit.

Speaking of weddings, the Rowlands family did a double take. We geared up for a double wedding in July. Not only did Brianna marry Eric, but after seven long years as a bachelor, I tied the matrimonial knot myself. My beautiful bride is Juliana Pagliarulo, a talented performer like her son. That's right, she's Antonio's mother. And, Juliana's daughter, Belina, moved in with us, too — a quiet, gentle girl — and I've grown to love her as if she were my own.

This Christmas we are celebrating not only two summer weddings and the addition of two grandchildren to our family, but we are also rejoicing over two Christmas engagements. Two weeks ago, Belina announced her engagement to Wesley Hopkins, the minister of music at our church. I've never seen Belina look more radiant.

On Christmas Eve, as all of my daughters and their families gathered for our holiday celebration, my youngest, Frannie, announced her engagement to real estate mogul Scott Winslow. They seem very much in love and have expressed their desire to serve God together in whatever way He leads.

Frannie and Belina are considering a double wedding in June. Of course, they want me to officiate, and I couldn't be more honored. Now I just have to figure out how to walk two brides down the aisle at once!

My dear friends, I'm not a man given easily to tears. But my heart is filled to overflowing this Christmas season as I think of the ways God has blessed our family. On Christmas morning, as we all gathered around the tree to open gifts, I realized that the good Lord had already given me the best gifts of all — His love revealed in the birth of a Babe in Bethlehem, and the enduring love of my cherished family.

Amid the laughter and chatter, the baby cries and child squeals, the carols and feasts and presents and prayers, I thank God for His great abundance to us. I have so much to rejoice over — the precious memory of Mandy and her caring influence on our family; my devoted wife, Juliana, who delights me with her spontaneity and spirit; and my three — no, four — exquisite daughters who have found the men of their dreams and are creating their own happy families.

Maybe it's time for me to settle back and relax a bit, now that each of my girls has someone to watch over her. I'm not getting any younger, so I suppose it's time to leave the matchmaking ploys to someone else. Then again, with the grandchildren coming, maybe I'd better keep on my toes. I want to be sure the next generation has a taste of all the joys and happiness our family has known.

Wishing you the Spirit of Christmas all year long,

Andrew Rowlands (and his bountiful brood!)

CAROLE GIFT PAGE writes from the heart about issues facing women today. A prolific author of over 40 books and 800 stories and articles, she has published both fiction and nonfiction with a dozen major Christian publishers, including Thomas Nelson, Moody Press, Crossway Books, Bethany House, Tyndale House and Harvest House. An award-winning novelist, Carole has received the C. S. Lewis Honor Book Award and been a finalist several times for the prestigious Gold Medallion Award and the Campus Life Book of the Year Award.

A frequent speaker at churches, conferences, conventions, schools and retreats around the country, Carole shares her testimony (based on her inspiring new book. *Becoming a Woman of Passion*) and encourages women everywhere to discover and share their deepest passions, to keep passion alive on the home front and to unleash their passion for Christ.

Born and raised in Jackson, Michigan, Carole taught creative writing at Biola University in La Mirada, California, and serves on the advisory board of the American Christian Writers. She and her husband, Bill, live in Southern California and have three children (besides Misty in heaven) and three beautiful grandchildren.

The employees of Thorndike Press hope you have enjoyed this Large Print book. All our Thorndike and Wheeler Large Print titles are designed for easy reading, and all our books are made to last. Other Thorndike Press Large Print books are available at your library, through selected bookstores, or directly from us.

For information about titles, please call:

(800) 223-1244

or visit our Web site at:

www.gale.com/thorndike
www.gale.com/wheeler

To share your comments, please write:

Publisher
Thorndike Press
295 Kennedy Memorial Drive
Waterville, ME 04901